BOYFRIEND WITH BENEFITS

ALLISON TEMPLE

BOYFRIEND WITH BENEFITS

When Bailey's new boss turns out to be his childhood bully, a.k.a. Jake the Jerk, it's time to call in backup for the annual corporate retreat in Vegas. Too bad Bailey works too much to date. His best option is to ask his very straight roommate to play the part of temporary boyfriend, even if Gordo is better with pythons than he is with people.

But they haven't even checked into the hotel and Jake the Jerk is already everywhere. The pressure is on for Bailey to prove he deserves to climb the corporate ladder, but it's hard to talk shop when Gordo goes from backup to an increasingly attractive distraction.

Bailey's trying to keep his cool, schmooze the executives, and stick to the plan, even though Gordo's not playing by any of the rules. They've always been just friends, but maybe it's time to be boyfriends . . . with full benefits.

Boyfriend with Benefits is a 37k contemporary MM romance novella. It features fake boyfriends who might not be so fake, a hotel room with only one bed, and a James Bond moment in a tiny blue bathing suit. HEA guaranteed.

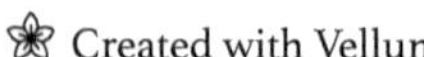 Created with Vellum

Cover Design: Cate Ashwood Designs
Editing: Posy Roberts, Boho Press
Proofreading: Kiki Clark, LesCourt Author Services

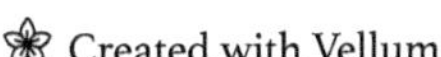 Created with Vellum

For the Muskoka retreat crew.
This book would not exist without you.
Team Gordo FTW!

For news on future releases, join the A-List, my monthly newsletter (allisontemplebooks.com/newsletter)

1

———

The word *nemesis* gets thrown around a lot.

And yet, on Tuesday morning, when the company-wide email with the merger announcement gets sent out and then we're all shuffled into the conference room so we can meet the "new" Senior Vice President of North American Sales, sometimes *nemesis* is the only word that fits.

Because standing there in a pearly grey suit, pink shirt, and a smirk that would curdle milk, is Jake Kenyon.

Better known as Jake the Jerk.

Except no one knows that but me. Because no one else had ten years of their life made a waking nightmare by the new SVP NAS except for me. He's introduced by Lachlan, our Regional VP, who seems awed to be in Jake's presence.

"I know it's been a different kind of morning," Lachlan says. "But I promise you your jobs are all safe and the company is heading in a very exciting direction."

I tune out. He's basically reciting what was in the email word for word. Strategic growth. New opportunity. Blah, blah, blah. When I read the memo—okay, I skimmed most of it—the only thing I checked closely was the revised org chart. I interviewed two and a half weeks ago for the VP of New Account Acquisition position, and I was terrified that the merger meant the job was gone.

It was. My name drew a straight line to Lachlan's, and then right above him was Jake the Jerk's.

Except, at the time, all I thought was *"Huh. I used to know a Jake Kenyon. Isn't that weird?"* Because what were the odds that the bully who lived down the street from me as a kid and spent every hour he could trying to steal my bike, throw rocks at me through the fence, run me down with his car once he got his learner's permit, and basically torment me in any way imaginable, would now be my boss's boss? He'd moved away while we were still in high school. Somewhere across the country, and I never heard from him again.

Speaking of hearing, the boardroom has gone quiet. I blink back to reality and everyone is staring at me.

"Excuse me, what?" I say, because clearly I've been asked a question or something. Several guys around the table are shifting nervously, and Jake's eyeing me, so I sit up straighter in my chair. I've got my phone in my lap, and a message pops up on the screen.

Stand up, say who you are, what your position is, and stop making me look like an asshole.

It's from Lachlan, who is glaring daggers at his laptop.

I push up to my feet. The twenty faces in the room are all watching me. I'm watching Jake the Jerk as I very clearly say, "Bailey Baldwin, Regional Associate VP of Sales."

And so I see—also very clearly—the moment recognition hits. The smirk turns predatory. Women and children flee in front of it . . . if there were any women or children present today, but no, the sales department at the Toronto office of Blaumann, Glick, Schuler & Maxwell International is a sausage fest.

"Nice to meet you," Jake says.

"I'm also Salesperson of the Year for the last three years running, and I designed our Smart Challenge sales process, which saw our closure rate increase by fifteen percent last year."

Jake's eyes narrow, and that little addition was a mistake. He knows he's caught me off guard and I'm trying to build up fortifications when the army's already at the gate.

The rest of the meeting is . . . I don't know. I'm sure they talk about KPIs and compensation packages. Lachlan says something about an upcoming retreat for everyone at the Ass VP (that's what I like to call myself) level and up to discuss future planning. A few people are even smiling as we file out again.

All I can think is that I'm so relieved that it doesn't sound as if Jake is going be around much. BGS&M has offices all over the country and North America. He's responsible for sales and marketing for all of them, but it sounds like he's working out of what is now the head office.

As I go back to my cubicle, I pull out my phone and bring up Gordo's number. He's at home today—he's at home most days—and he needs to know I'll be coming in hot after work.

Big shake up at the office. Get snacks. And tequila.

Two cupcake emojis come back in reply. I don't know if that means he's going to bake cupcakes. I was thinking more like cannabis brownies, but whatever floats his boat. Gordo is a born and bred mother hen. He bakes his own sourdough, mills his own soap, and fosters reptiles that people get as pets and then realize aren't nearly as fun as a golden retriever. Last summer we had a fourteen-foot python at our condo, but surprisingly, the demand for pythons is high, and Piña Colada was only with us for a week before she went to her forever home.

"Bailey." My name on the air has all the warmth of a snake's hiss in January. I glance over my shoulder and Jake the Jerk is there.

"Oh. Hey," I say, like I've just run into him in the aisles at

Wal-Mart. Although, judging from the way his suit fits him as he pulls off his jacket, he hasn't been inside a Wal-Mart in the last decade.

I'm also pleased his growth spurt never fully kicked in after he left town. I'm on the small side of five nine, but Jake probably tells people he's five eight when we both know he's five six and a half tops.

His eyes narrow. "It's good to see you."

Piña Colada could give him some tips on putting out friendly vibes.

I say, "Yeah, you too."

He says, "It's so funny. When I saw your name on the org chart, I thought it couldn't possibly be you, but here you are."

I laugh. "And here *you* are!"

He moves into my space, which forces me to take a step back, retreating into my cubicle. I set my laptop down on its stand so it looks like that's what I meant to do all along.

"I hope there won't be any . . ." He bites the inside of his cheek.

"Any what?" I say sweetly.

"Hard feelings. You know. From when we were kids."

"You mean when you outed me to my entire family?"

He shrugs. "I thought they knew. You spent all your time hanging around with me."

Two clarifications here:

1. I did not spend all my time "hanging around" with him. I spent all my time trying to get away from him as he tormented me and harassed me, but my parents took a "boys will be boys" view of it and assumed we were friends.

2. Jake's as gay as I am, but that doesn't mean anything, either about him or me. I know the obvious assumption here is that he was even more closeted than I was in his teenage years and that he worked out his internalized homophobia on me, because

those are the bully stories we hear, but no. Jake was out by the time he grew his first chin hair. By age sixteen, he was taking guys like Ethan Whittier to the homecoming dance. And somewhere along the way, he took a picture of me kissing Billy Marsh in the back alley behind our house and left it in our mailbox for my parents to find, then sashayed on home to draw hearts around *JK & EW 4Ever*. Not every bully has a tragic Lifetime movie back story. Sometimes a bully is simply a bully.

But . . . boys will be boys, right?

My lip curls. I can't help it. The shocked look on my dad's face when he pulled the picture out of the mail—seriously, how could he not have seen me coming? I knew all the words to every musical number on *Glee,* and I was in the process of mastering the choreography when Jake dropped off his love note—was the beginning of years of awkwardness between us that we are only getting over lately, and it's all Jake's fault. I would have come out to them eventually, but in my own time and my own way.

"What a weird little alien you are." I give him the kind of smile people use when they've insulted someone but want anyone out of earshot to think we're having a good laugh together.

His sneer is similar as he steps farther into my cubicle. "Takes one to know one."

"Ooo," I hiss. "Burn. Are you going to tell me you're rubber and I'm glue next?"

Jake's smile turns evil. He fixes the button at the cuff of his pink shirt. He says, "Bailey, don't be a bitch because you didn't get the promotion. It was never going to happen. We all have to tighten our belts."

How? How does he know about that? How did this become my life in the turn of an email? There are millions of people in this city, millions more in this country, and I now work for Jake the Jerk.

I say, "I didn't want it anyway. Lachlan convinced me to try. But look at you. Big man on campus. Hope you enjoy travelling forty-six weeks a year."

We both know I'm lying. Lachlan's told me about his benefits package before, and I can only assume Jake's is the same or better. He gets at least four weeks of vacation, and all the travel to visit the teams who now report to him means he'll have enough frequent flyer points to spend a whole month in Bora Bora if he wants to, every single year.

I would love to go to Bora Bora.

I glance at my screensaver. Gordo and I are smiling back at me, with the badlands in the distance. Not the real badlands. We didn't go to South Dakota. We went to Caledon, an hour north of here. And you aren't allowed to go into the park anymore because people are assholes and ignore signs that say, *Please stay off the ancient geological formations*, and now we can't have nice things. We didn't know that, though, when we picked up the Zipcar and drove out of the city. We thought we were going on an adventure. The badlands. Where men are men and rattlesnakes are ... well ... okay, they're pretty manly too. Gordo was especially excited about the snakes. And then we got there and it was closed, and I made Gordo take the selfie anyway, so we could pretend the whole thing wasn't a waste of time.

"That your boyfriend?" Jake asks. I rip my gaze away from the screen to catch his smirk, like he thinks there's no way I could be with someone.

Thank you, Gordo, for always being there when I need you.

"Yes," I say. "Yes, he is. We live together, actually."

"What's he do?" Jake asks, because of course he does. He would never start with something so practical as "What's his name?" or "Where did you meet?" All he wants to know is if I was able to snag someone worthy of his attention.

"He's a rocket scientist," I say quickly. "Literally. He builds rocket engines for Rolls-Royce. He was headhunted by Elon Musk last year for SpaceX, but he's got standards, so he turned them down."

Jake purses his lips. He's probably trying to extrapolate, based on all the other people he's judged in his lifetime, what a Rolls-Royce rocket scientist makes and whether it's so much he can't make fun of me.

You may be wondering how I know Rolls-Royce makes rocket engines. Gordo has a thing for those "how it's made" YouTube videos. We watch a lot of them.

Also, everything I said above is a lie. He is not a rocket scientist. Gordo is . . . well, he pays his rent on time, but don't ask me how, because he definitely doesn't work a nine to five. Sometimes he's at home and sometimes he's not, but I have no idea where he goes or what he does all day when I'm at work. When I ask, he says things like "Stuff" and "Slept" and "I started a petition to end the illegal wildlife trade in Oklahoma, we already have three thousand signatures, do you know anyone else who might sign it?" But none of that sounds like it makes any money.

And he's not my boyfriend. Loyal, committed roommate, that's all. I maybe thought about it once or twice, but I knew it was never going to happen the first time we watched a Marvel movie and he sympathetically told me how terrible he felt about the raw deal Scarlett Johansson's character gets throughout the series.

"She deserves so much better," he said with sparkling tears in his eyes.

Any guy who worships at the altar of ScarJo is too straight for me.

"Are you with anyone?" I ask, trying to draw Jake's attention off the picture of Gordo and surprising myself with my own boldness. When we were kids, I'd have never asked him a direct question like that.

"Elias," he says with a smile. "He farms emus."

I have no idea how much an emu farmer makes. Or what exactly he would farm them for.

"Sounds cozy," I say.

"You'll meet him at the retreat," Jake says, and my blood goes cold. I didn't give the retreat any thought when Lachlan mentioned it. I'd been invited to a few in the past, but they were always very "employees only," and that suited me fine. Too hard to get hammered at the bar in the evenings if you're with someone.

But if Jake's bringing Emu Elias, that may have to change.

"Well, he and Gord—" I stutter over his name. I can't tell him my supposed boyfriend's name is Gordo. He'll never let me live that down. "Gordon will have a chance to hang out." I gently punch Jake's shoulder, like we've been bonding this whole time. Inside, I hope I wrinkle his perfect shirt, but of course it's made from some space-age material that doesn't even show the impression of my knuckles. Whoever designed it probably does know Elon Musk.

He laughs. It's a short percussive sound that he perfected in grade school. I've had nightmares about it, but I can't let him smell my fear.

He says, "I look forward to working with you, Bailey."

He might as well say, "Lockers. Three thirty. If you don't show up, remember I know where you live."

Once he leaves, I sag down into my seat, letting it roll gently to a stop as it takes my weight.

I am so fucked. I have spent the last nine years climbing the ladder at BGS&M, and even if they swear my job is safe after this merger, there's no way in hell I can survive working with Jake the Jerk.

I pick up my phone and text Gordo.

Those cupcakes better be fucking magical.

2

———

My roommate is a lifesaver.

"You're the best person I know," I say from where I'm sprawled on the couch.

Look at what he made for me!

Gordo's cupcakes really are amazing, with exactly the right amount of THC baked in. For a moment, I forget all about Jake the Jerk. Also, my verbal filter is functioning at about half capacity, but as far as I know, Gordo is a human cone of silence, so it's never been a problem.

Gordo's in the leather armchair across from me. A bearded dragon named Bernard is sitting on his shoulder glaring at me. Bernard hasn't liked me since he moved in a month ago. I'm not sure what I ever did to him, but we have agreed to keep our space. He thinks Gordo is the shit though, as do I right now.

Gordo smiles at me. "Thanks. I used too much butter in the frosting."

I got home from work feeling like I was about ready to have a heart attack. Then the sweet scent of vanilla and lemon wafted through the door as I walked into the condo and all the stress melted off me. Gordo was in the kitchen putting the finishing touches on his cupcakes, and for a split second, I envied him so much. He was wearing his favourite apron, tied around his waist, along with a backwards ball cap, stretched out T-shirt, and a pair of cut-off shorts that haven't been cut off evenly, so one of his pale freckled legs looks significantly longer than the other. This is basically Gordo's uniform—although the apron comes and goes—and in comparison, my button-down and pressed pants felt like they were about to choke me.

But everything is better with Gordo's special cupcakes.

"Like really, no one else I know has a roommate who bakes for them," I say. We've got Netflix playing but I'll be damned if I know what's on. Some kind of teenage love-triangle thing. I want to tell them all they're sixteen and shouldn't be taking this so seriously. Move on. Find other frogs to kiss.

Speaking of, Gordo makes kissing noises as Bernard butts his spiky head under Gordo's chin. Have I mentioned that Gordo is a giant? I live with a fricking Viking. He's easily six six and must weigh close to three hundred pounds and literally blocks out the sun when he comes through a door. Combined with his mat of red hair, and you might as well call him Svendal the Terror or whatever.

"Well, you said you had a rough day." He lifts a pair of tweezers, and Bernard goes into his ready pose as the cricket Gordo is holding squirms.

I wince. "Could you not do that here?"

I don't mind Gordo's hobbies. In fact, they're kind of cool. Once upon a time, I thought I'd get a cat or something, but I'm not home even enough to take care of a fuzzy killer who lives on dry kibble and shits in a box. So having Gordo's menagerie around is nice. I just don't like it when he turns our living room into Wild Kingdom.

Gordo smiles at me. "No problem." He tickles Bernard under

his chin. "You're probably starting to get cold anyway, aren't you?"

He stands and stretches. The front of his shirt rides up, exposing his hairy belly. I stare longer than I should, but I can only blame Gordo's baking for my lack of social boundaries. Guys built like him are my catnip. Obviously not *Gordo*. Even if he were a little curious, fucking your roommate is never a good idea. But he's nice enough to look at, even if his fashion sense is painfully heterosexual. Jersey and cargo shorts in the summer, jersey and more jersey in the winter. Sometimes he'll put on jeans if he's leaving the house. No one would ever mistake him for a social media style influencer, that's for sure.

Gordo and I met two years ago, after my last break up. I suddenly had a downtown condo I couldn't afford to live in by myself, and I was too busy at work to look for somewhere new. So I did what any self-respecting millennial would do: I put a call out for a roommate on social media. Gordo was a friend of a friend of a friend, but he promised to do his share of the cooking and cleaning as long as I let him bring his animals into the place, and that seemed like a fair deal.

"Are we watching another one?" he asks as he crosses in front of the TV with Bernard riding his shoulder. The screen has that obnoxious *Are you still there?* message on it. Fuck you, Netflix. Don't judge my life choices.

"Sure." I smile up at him as I reach for another cupcake.

Sooo . . .

I kinda forget to mention the retreat to Gordo. I mean, I did ask for something to get my mind off work, and his treats did an incredibly effective job. I only wish I'd remembered to hold onto the "Jake thinks I have a boyfriend" part of my tale of woe for a little longer. But, whatever, I'll tell him when I get home the next day.

Then everything at the office goes to hell.

Jake suddenly runs my life. There are daily emails from him to the entire North American sales department, and then a whole subset sent directly to me and Lachlan for us to distribute to our respective teams. They use phrases like "checking in" and "circling back" and "measurable expectations" like this is our first rodeo. Friend, this isn't even my second rodeo. I have belt buckles that would give you curvature of the spine.

Incidentally, it turns out that our North American sales department is getting smaller by the day. While all our jobs are safe at my office, the same is not true elsewhere. More memos get sent from the new HR department with words like "consolidation" and "difficult decision." I may not get the New Account Acquisition job, but suddenly I am responsible for a whole shit ton of prospect accounts that weren't mine before. The mood at work shifts from nervously optimistic to strung out and terrified. I'm pretty sure Lachlan has stopped going home and has a cot hidden under his desk that he pulls out and sleeps on while he tries to keep his entire team from quitting on him.

Also, Gordo disappears for a few days. I come home and there's a note on the front door that says *Please feed Bernard. Crickets in the pantry. Use tweezers so they don't all escape.*

I hate the crickets. No matter what Gordo says about tweezers, I know at least a few have gone rogue and set up hideouts in our ductwork. You can hear the occasional ominous chirp in the middle of the night, like they want you to know they're still out there and they know what you did to the rest of their cricket family.

In any case, I do my best, and Bernard grudgingly chomps on his meal while giving me the evil eye, and I'm so caught up by surviving my job and not getting murdered in my sleep by vengeful crickets that I forget about the whole retreat thing again when Gordo gets back.

We're less than a week from departure when an email comes

into my inbox. Jake's name is on it and I almost delete it, because I just *can't* anymore with him today, but the subject line is: *When do you arrive?* and for a minute, I think I've missed a meeting. My heart drops when I click it open.

Bailey,

Elias and I are looking forward to seeing you and Gordon at the retreat. We're flying in on Thursday at noon. Do you have time for drinks on Thursday afternoon?

Jake Kenyon

Senior Vice President, North American Sales

Shit. Shit, shit, shit.

What a passive-aggressive asshole.

But also, what are my possible responses here? My flight isn't scheduled to get in until later on Thursday night, so I can decline, but then what? He'll suggest we get together for breakfast and I'll have to dodge that too. Poor Gordo has food poisoning from the room-temperature roast beef sandwich he bought on the plane. Then he's got allergies from the desert dust and can't leave his room. An endless cycle of lies.

So I do the only thing I possibly can.

I go home prepared to beg.

No notes about chameleons. When I open the door, Gordo's in the kitchen, his back to me.

Seeing him is a relief. He'll always help a friend in need—or that's what I tell myself—and I am very much in need.

"I have a big favour to ask," I say. I can't help the way I pull my knees up against me as I try to casually settle onto the couch. Hiding my vital organs in case Gordo decides to rip me a new one seems advisable.

"Okay." He turns and he's holding a bowl of what looks like recently hydrated Cup O' Noodles.

"And you're going to want to say no, but please hear me out."

There's a drop of noodle broth—is it really broth if it was

water from the kettle five minutes ago?—in his beard, and he wipes it away as he says, "I'll keep that in mind."

"I need you to come to the retreat with me this weekend."

He frowns. When Gordo frowns, his whole face basically disappears. His mouth burrows under his beard, his eyes get lost beneath the caterpillars he calls eyebrows, and his forehead scrunches up so his shaggy hair covers most of the rest of him. He's a nose surrounded by a forest of red fur.

Also, he's looming, which he doesn't mean to do, but when you're as big as he is, it's easy to make people uncomfortable.

He says, "You want me to come to your corporate retreat this weekend?"

I nod, and the second part of what I have to say gets stuck on my tongue, turning it thick and fuzzy the way that fancy French red wine that Lachlan likes to serve at this supper club he hosts does—or used to, back before he moved into the office.

I swallow and wait for my saliva to come back before I blurt out the rest of my request. "And I need you to pretend to be my boyfriend."

For a while, he doesn't say anything. In fact, he lifts the bowl of noodles again and slurps in a few big bites. My stomach goes to acid and my toes curl up in my socks. He's going to say no, and I'm so doomed. I'll have to face Jake by myself and admit that I lied.

"You want me to be your boyfriend?" he says.

"Pretend, yeah. Just for the weekend."

"Why?"

Oh God. So terrible. This is the worst, but I'm literally out of time. "Because Jake will be there."

Gordo nods like he was expecting that. "Jake the Jerk?"

"Yeah." I moan and flop over onto the couch, covering my face with a throw cushion. "And he kinda already thinks we're dating."

"I'm sorry." Gordo slurps on more noodles. "I didn't hear that last part clearly behind the pillow. It sounded like you said we're dating."

I push the pillow aside and glare at him. "I said he *thinks* we're dating."

"Why would he think that?"

So embarrassing. My instincts are still telling me to cover myself. That it's only a matter of time before I get eviscerated, and I'll probably deserve it too.

But Gordo's not actually like that. What he is, though, is waiting for an answer, and I can't expect him to play along if he doesn't have all the information.

"Because it's possible I told him you were my boyfriend." I stare up at him, pleading silently for him not to freak out.

Instead, he smacks his lips. "Bailey, I think I'd remember if I had a boyfriend."

Would he though? Sometimes I don't know what gets Gordo out of bed in the morning, or how he manages to have mostly clean clothes every day. He's this lumbering mountain of a man —emphasis on lumbering—who seems to roll through life with all the self-determination of a Thanksgiving Day parade balloon.

"Well, you've got one now," I say, giving him awkward jazz hands.

He studies me. I feel incredibly vulnerable, lying on the couch while he towers over me. He's going to laugh. He's going to call me a drama queen. He's going to tell me he has plans this weekend.

He says, "Where is it again?"

Hope sparks to life. I grip the cushion until my knuckles turn white. "Vegas."

He wrinkles his nose. "Sounds tacky."

"Please, Gordo." I tumble to the floor and crawl to him on my knees. "Please. You'd be the best friend in the world. I'll do anything you want. I will wash the dishes, I will feed the turtles. They can live in my room if you want. Please, Gordo, I am begging you. You don't even have to do anything. Come to some dinners, hang out by the pool, and keep me from drowning Jake. No funny business. No kissing, no touching. We will be the most platonic boyfriends ever."

"What if I don't want to?" he says, scratching his belly.

"Please." I clasp my hands together. Catholic martyrs have nothing on Bailey Baldwin when he's desperate. "I don't know what else to do."

He slurps the last of his noodles, chewing thoughtfully. I'm still on the floor. I will not rise until he has saved my bacon.

Finally, he says, "Yeah, okay."

"Okay?" The relief that rushes through me makes my whole body go weak until I topple over. From here, I could basically kiss Gordo's toes. They're bare, in a pair of flip flops, but before I can reach for them, he walks away, taking his bowl to the kitchen where he carefully washes it out. I've managed to get back onto the couch by the time he returns.

"I want to see the fountains," he says.

"The fountains?"

"Yeah." He rocks on the balls of his feet, looking sheepish, which is no mean feat when you're the approximate size and shape of a garden shed. "You see them in movies. There's lights and music."

"At the Bellagio?" I say.

He shrugs. "Is that in Vegas? Because I want to see the fountains in Vegas."

I can't tell if he's joking. Or he's making a dig about the time we went to the badlands that weren't the real badlands.

That trip has gotten me into so much trouble.

"Sure," I say. "We can go see the fountains."

"And the horses."

Now I've lost what he's talking about. "What horses?"

"They have wild mustangs in Nevada. I had a book about them when I was little." His whole face lights up, the way it always does when he starts talking about animals.

"Yes, Gordo." I sigh. "We can see the mustangs too." I have no idea how one does that, but for Gordo, my new fake boyfriend and all-around best friend, I will figure it out.

"I'll go book a flight," Gordo says, like it's all been decided.

"I'll send you the details on mine. Let's try to fly together." Not that it matters. Jake is coming in from the West Coast. We only need to be a couple once we hit the ground. But as I scroll through my email to find my flight confirmation and send it to Gordo, I see Jake's email, and I can't help it when I go back to it and hit Reply.

Jake,

So sorry, but Gordon and I won't be arriving until later in the evening. Let's try breakfast?

Best,

Bailey Baldwin

Regional Ass. VP Sales & Marketing

We're going to rock this retreat.

3

———

The rest of the workweek sucks. The merger announcement was full of sweet words about how there wouldn't be too many changes. And in fact, the word "change" never gets used. But there sure are a lot of "operational enhancements" flying around. For example, Lachlan passes down new sales targets that mean I'll have to work two hundred hours a week for the rest of the year if I want a hope in hell of hitting them.

On Thursday, I still have so much left to do that I pack up my clothes and other shit and put it by the door to take to the office with me so I can go directly to the airport instead of coming home.

"Flight leaves at seven," I say to Gordo, who is warming up frozen mice in the microwave. We have another python in residence, but she's going to a different foster this afternoon. "So we want to be at the airport at five. Terminal three. You're going to remember."

"Terminal three," he says, poking a mouse with a chopstick. I try to be gone before he starts this part of his routine. Something about it makes my stomach turn. I'm running late this morning because of the extra time it took to pack.

"Five o'clock. Gordo, you're listening, right?"

He glances up, and when he makes eye contact, it's like my whole being distills down to a single ball of light.

Look, I'll be the first to admit that I'm a little . . . high strung. It's part of my charm and definitely part of what's made me successful at work. Sales is a tough racket, and when I've got a good prospect, I'm like a Jack Russell Terrier on speed. Won't take no for an answer? I won't even let it get to a no.

But somehow, when Gordo looks at me—which isn't very often, he's much more of a "looking at a point two inches above your head" kind of guy, as though he's surprised anyone else is in the room at all—something inside me stops spinning. It's almost a relief, like I've been waiting for an opportunity to chill.

But this morning, I don't need to chill. I need to get to work.

"Bailey," Gordo says, "I'll be there."

And I have to trust he will.

Of course, I leave my stuff by the door. I text Gordo in a panic and ask him to bring it all with him. His reply is a complicated series of emojis that might be confirmation that he'll do it but might also be a question as to whether or not I think he'll get held up at customs if he brings a live (or possibly stuffed? It's unclear.) iguana in his carry-on luggage. Gordo's never been much of a talker, but sometimes I wish he'd use a few more words.

Work is hellacious. I can't believe they're sending so many of the sales team to Vegas for the weekend when conditions on the ground are this chaotic, but when I mention it to Lachlan as we collide in the kitchen—I'm on my fifth coffee of the day—he shrugs and says his plan is to drink on the company dime for as many consecutive hours as he can over the next three days.

And then Jake sends me a meeting invite—*a fucking meeting*

invite—with the subject line "Couples Breakfast" for tomorrow. Seriously? Who puts a cozy romantic breakfast into Outlook next to "Ice Breaker 1" and "Sales of the Future: Masterclass"?

I leave it unanswered. Let him wonder if I'm actually coming.

No, I correct myself, if *we're* coming.

There's a truck rolled over on the highway, so I'm twenty minutes late to the airport. I rush through sliding doors and dodge past families with wheelie suitcases that look like they must carry everything they own. I catch sight of Gordo's red hair, and a tiny fraction of the stress I'm carrying eases out.

"Hey buddy, are you—" My question cuts off when I take a look at the luggage around him. They're all mine. "Where's your stuff?"

He gives me a relaxed smile and swings to show me the ratty backpack hanging off one of his massive shoulders. "In here."

I gape. The damn thing wouldn't hold the shoes I've brought —and I've only packed three pairs.

"Gordo." I take a deep breath to keep calm. He's in his usual uniform—ninety percent jersey, none of it purchased new or in this decade—and suddenly I'm imagining him, seated across the table from Jake and his emu farmer boyfriend. Somehow, I don't think the boyfriend will be there in his overalls.

Was this a bad idea?

"This is a corporate retreat," I say. "Professional. Did you at least bring a suit?"

"No." He laughs like the answer is obvious.

I close my eyes. We talked about this. I went over the entire itinerary with him and printed him off a copy so I could highlight the events he'd need to come to. And yes, Gordo's not a details guy, but I sort of assumed he'd absorb enough information to get a sense of the dress code, even if he couldn't tell you where we're eating dinner every night.

A big hand comes down on my shoulder, nearly knocking

me off my feet. But when I open my eyes, Gordo's smiling merrily down at me.

"Don't worry, Bailey." He always has this subtext whenever he says my name that makes me think he's hearing the words "silly human" in his head. "I'm here to make you look good, and I'm going to do it."

I wish I could be so certain.

But he's taken a good first step—wardrobe choices aside—because he's already checked us into our flight, so all I have to do is drop off my bags, and we hurry down halls and over walkways until we're in line for security.

Gordo, as it turns out, has not brought a live lizard, so that's good. He does have a rather large unmarked Tupperware with something white and runny in his bag though.

"It's shampoo," he says with a smile to the security agent. "I made it myself."

I sigh some more, as the agent asks him about volumes and Ziploc bags, and he tells her he doesn't know how much is in the container, but would she like the recipe?

He looks pretty upset when she makes him throw his home-made shampoo away.

Honestly, I'm not real happy about it either. I've snuck some a few times when I'm out of my own store-bought stuff, and it leaves my hair smelling amazing.

"When was the last time you flew somewhere?" I ask. I thought everyone knew about the whole "nothing but tiny bottles" rule.

Gordo shrugs. "I don't really like to fly. I took the train to Salt Lake City last summer."

I trip over my feet as I try to do up my shoelaces. "When were you in Salt Lake City?"

He shakes his head, chuckling. "Last summer. I just told you."

That's how most conversations with Gordo go. He is the king of living in the moment. I got on a wellness kick early last year where I tried to meditate every day. My best streak was three days, and when I suggested to Gordo he might do it too for moral support, he said he didn't need to meditate, and I'm pretty sure he's right. Whether he can attribute his "live your best life" attitude to life experience or heavy consumption of medicinals, I'll never know.

We don't have time to stop at the airport bar. Our gate is the very last one at the end of a concourse with fifty-seven possibilities, and as we arrive, a cheery gate agent is announcing pre-boarding for all first-class passengers.

"Come on." Gordo grabs my hand and pulls me forward.

"No." I shake my head. "That's not us. We have to wait for the gen-pop seating."

I fucking hate flying. Being squashed like cattle into itty-bitty seats with itty-bittier tray tables too small to hold my laptop. I lose so many hours of productivity when I'm travelling. Between having no room on the plane and nowhere to plug in a charger while I wait at the gate, the whole process is hugely inefficient.

But meanwhile, Gordo is still tugging me toward the line of passengers boarding.

"Gordo, we're not—this isn't—we're—" I glance at my ticket to confirm our zone number and squint before I realize it says very clearly, "First Class."

Whaaaat?

I gape like a Minion as Gordo walks us up to the counter, hands the woman there our tickets and IDs, and then leads me down the jetway and onto the plane.

First class is . . .

I let Gordo stash my laptop bag in the overhead bin as I settle down into the wide leather seat that wouldn't be out of place in front of my TV.

First class is *nice.*

"Gordo," I hiss, eyeing flight attendants as they move up and down the aisles. "These aren't our seats."

He pats my hand and grins. "Sure they are."

"No they aren't." I distinctly remember buying the cheapest ticket I could, because as much as I've enjoyed working there until recently, BGS&M has some truly draconian travel expense policies.

He pats me again, and I half expect him to tell me not to worry my pretty little head. But before he can say anything else, a flight attendant is asking us about our in-flight beverage preferences, and we're pulling away from the gate.

My in-flight beverage preference is a manhattan with extra cherries, and the crew delivers it in spades. Gordo asks for a tomato juice, and once we've been served, he holds his glass out —*real glass.* I thought it was plastic everywhere on these flying cigar tubes—and waits for me to tap mine against it.

"To you," he says.

"Me?" I can't help my smile. He's doing that looking-at-me thing again that always makes me feel fluttery. Once upon a time, when he first moved in, I hoped maybe we had a shot. But two years later, I'm glad we've found a way to coexist, even if I don't get to rub myself all over that bushy red beard.

"You've been so stressed lately. I hope you find a chance to unwind this weekend," he says.

I flush. "I'm sorry if I've been grumpy." I've been more than grumpy. But Gordo's my roommate, not my mom. He doesn't need to listen to me bitch about things.

He pulls the little plastic sword out of my drink and drags one of the cherries off with his teeth.

"Those are mine!" I say, louder than is strictly socially appropriate on an airplane.

Gordo grins as he chews. "I'll make it up to you."

Truthfully, he already has, just by being here.

The flight's pretty good. We should never fly anything but first class. I'll ask Lachlan about it when we get back. Of course, my general enjoyment might come from the three manhattans I have before we're even over the Midwest. And the fact that the in-flight entertainment includes a Marvel marathon, and Steve Rogers's ass is *fine*, even on an eight-inch screen at 35,000 feet. Gordo sits next to me, watching some independent film with subtitles I don't recognize. He's always watching things like that.

I'm asleep when we land, and I jolt awake as the plan lurches and decelerates on the runway.

"Hi," Gordo says, voice quiet even over the roar of plane engines.

"Hey." The inside of my mouth tastes like festering maraschino cherries and I regret that.

"We're here," he says.

"Yeah." I scrunch up my face and glance out the window. The sun is setting in Las Vegas, and lights swoop and twinkle on the horizon. My pulse picks up. I've been to Vegas a few times, and it's always fun.

I bump my shoulder against Gordo's, which is a trick given the wide seat arm between us, and smile. He smiles back. The canned voice over the PA system welcomes us to Las Vegas and says they hope we enjoy our stay.

Right now, looking at Gordo, I'm starting to think I will.

4

Nope, spoke too soon. Everything goes swimmingly as we get off our plane—good old first class means we don't have to wait for everyone else to disembark—but things go awry pretty quickly after that.

First off, Gordo's backpack literally falls apart. I don't even know how. But one second I'm walking up the concourse looking for the signs that will point us to baggage claim, and the next, Gordo's going, "Uh, Bailey," and when I turn around, he's staring at a pile of fabric on the floor between his feet, and the bottom seam of his backpack has completely come undone.

I can't even, but we stop at a "It Doesn't Have to Stay in Vegas" souvenir shop, and Gordo buys a rhinestone Elvis tote bag, and he seems pretty happy about it, and it's definitely an improvement over him carrying what few things he's brought for this weekend in a ball between his hands.

But I should have taken that incident as a warning.

My bags aren't even here. Which, I guess is marginally better than finding out my suit has been shredded on a conveyor belt somewhere, but only barely. We stand in line for the customer service counter for over an hour and a half.

"This is ridiculous," I mutter to myself.

"It's okay," Gordo says. He's munching on a chocolate bar that he bought along with his sparkly bag. "Everyone else here is frustrated, but it doesn't make the line move faster. In fact, it makes it move slower because they don't use their listening skills when they finally get to talk to someone."

Listening skills? What is this, kindergarten?

"Do you want something to eat?" He holds out a bag of salt-and-vinegar chips to me.

"No, thank you." I give him a tight smile and shuffle forward. The buzz from the drinks is wearing off, and in its wake, I'm left tired and annoyed. I want to go to the hotel, check in, and crash. I'm already thinking about Jake and work and how much I'm dreading putting on my rah-rah go-team face this weekend.

We finally get to the counter, and the woman won't even look at me when she says, "Can I help you?"

As if she doesn't know why we're here.

"My luggage didn't come," I say.

She takes my flight information. "What does your suitcase look like, sir?"

Somehow the question seems absurd. "What does it look like? It's a suitcase," I say through clenched teeth. "It's got zippers and wheels and a handle."

She doesn't blink. "If you can give us a better description, it will help us make sure we find the right one."

I open my mouth to answer, but a big hand presses into my chest, and Gordo steps in front of me.

"It's a black Samsonite. Four wheels on the bottom, three pockets on the front. The material is scratched on the back and patched with electrical tape. Also black suit bag. Tan-coloured trim and zippers shaped like seahorses."

Huh.

If you'd asked me how many wheels my suitcase had, I'd have said two.

The woman's making notes. I glance up at Gordo. "Thanks."

He smiles at me like it's no big deal. "You're welcome."

Eventually she gives us a form and says my bags will be here tomorrow afternoon at the latest. Not ideal, but we'll make it work.

As we walk away, I say, "I don't think my suitcase is patched with electrical tape."

"It wasn't," Gordo says. "I was worried the material was going to tear more, so I fixed it for you."

If only the same could be said of his backpack.

Our hotel is tucked in just behind the Strip. I breathe a sigh of relief when the cab lets us off in front of it and we get checked in with no problem.

"Here you go, sir," the clerk at the desk says as he hands us each a key card. "I've got you booked into a Lakeview suite with—"

"Bailey?"

Oh no. So close.

I turn slowly, and here comes Jake the Jerk. He's smiling like he can't believe we've run into each other.

"Jake. Hi." I do my best to play along.

"Are you just getting in?" he asks.

"Yeah," I say.

"How was your flight?"

What the fuck? Is he actually going to be nice to me this weekend?

"It was good. First class. You know. The only way to travel."

He smirks, and then his lips pop into a little O like he's remembered something. "Bailey, this is my partner, Elias."

And Elias is . . . whoa. Do all emu farmers look like that? He must be the cover model for Emus Quarterly, because he's got hair that looks like it's only ever styled by professionals and a tan too perfectly matched to his wardrobe to be new. He's wearing tapered linen pants with a crocodile belt and matching loafers. He is perfection on a stick.

"So nice to meet you." He holds a hand out to me with his knuckles facing up, like he might be expecting me to kiss it.

I shake it instead. "Likewise."

And then.

Oh no.

Jake and Elias are both smiling expectantly and glancing around the lobby. Elias says, "Jake said you were bringing someone too?"

And I turn, and there's Gordo, also waiting for me to say something, and I—

I don't think I can. He's there, in his cut-offs and his saggy T-shirt with the bacon neck, his dollar store flip flops, and his rhinestone Elvis and—

He takes a big step forward—all of Gordo's steps are big—and holds out one meaty hand. He says, "Hi. I'm Gord—

"Gordon!" I leap into action. "This is my boyfriend, Gordon."

Gordo shoots me a glance, but he shakes Jake and Elias's hands and says nice things about how I've told him a lot about them, and did they have a good trip? And the whole time, Jake and Elias are looking him up and down, and I want to die from embarrassment because we are so obviously outclassed by these two.

Sooner than is probably socially appropriate—but I have to get us out of here before Jake or Elias suggests we all go find a bar and have a drink—I grab hold of Gordo's hand and start to pull him away.

"We're going to head upstairs," I say, trying to look like the last thing I want to do is leave this happy little chit chat. "Jetlag's a bitch, you know."

Jake and Elias don't put up much fuss as I more or less drag Gordo across the lobby and toward the elevator.

The room is . . . well, BGS&M may have some weird policies about how much they're willing to pay for flights, but the block of rooms they booked for this retreat must be A-plus. The suite is nothing short of palatial, with a sunken living room and a giant sectional sofa that faces a flat-screen TV the size of the jumbotron.

There is, however, only one bed.

"No," I say, wishing I had a suitcase to drop in disbelief. "No, I called and asked for a room with two beds."

"Are you sure?" Gordo asks, setting his Elvis bag down on the luggage rack.

"Of course I did. Once you agreed to come, I called right away to add your name to the room and asked about an extra bed. It was a whole thing, because they said all the rooms with two beds were sold out in our corporate block. I had to beg them."

"It's okay," Gordo says. "I think there's plenty of room for the both of us."

There definitely is. The bed is a king size at least, and possibly bigger.

"But that's not the point," I say. "I asked for something and they didn't give it to me. And I promised you this wouldn't be weird. I can't ask you to sleep with me."

Gordo puts his hands on my shoulders and stares into my eyes. "It's fine, Bailey. We'll be fine."

I pout. "I could sleep on the sofa, I guess."

He picks me up. Literally one second my feet are on the ground, and the next thing I know, he's got an arm around my back and the other under my knees and he's swept me off those very same feet like I'm made of paper.

"Gordo!" I squawk. My cheek is squashed against his chest

and he's warm. Like a furnace. It makes me dizzy. "Put me down."

And he does. With one quick heft, I'm airborne, flying before I land in the middle of the giant bed with a muffled thump and one more squawk for good measure.

Seriously. There may be city-states smaller than this bed.

"See," Gordo says with a satisfied smile and his hands on his hips. "Lots of space." And I sort of think this means he's going to lie down too, but instead he walks into the living room and pulls back the massive floor-to-ceiling curtains.

Vegas sparkles in front of us, all lights and billboards and many, many people and—

"Bailey!" Gordo breathes, sounding awestruck. "Look. It's the fountains."

His words are so childlike, I'm compelled to get off the bed and come investigate. Sure enough, our windows face the fountains at the Bellagio, which are dancing and waving in front of us. Even from way up here, they're spectacular in the truest sense of the word. A spectacle. We stand in silence for a long time, shoulder to shoulder—or I guess technically we're shoulder to elbow since Gordo's shoulder is about the same place as my head—and watch the show.

Finally it goes dark. Gordo says, "Where did it go?"

I shrug. "Maybe they only have them on some of the time?" On my previous trips to Vegas, I was too blitzed or too asleep to pay attention to things like fountains.

He stares out the window forlornly. I pat his arm. "Don't worry, buddy. I'm sure we'll see them again."

I go to the bathroom to brush my teeth, using the complimentary toothbrush and paste the front desk gave us when I told them my tale of luggage woe. When I come back out, Gordo's still at the window.

"It's really big, isn't it?" he says.

"Yeah," I say, peeling off my clothes until I'm only in my underwear. "It definitely is."

I slide into the bed, and holy crap, this is not only the biggest thing I've ever slept in, it might also be the most comfortable. The pillow cradles my head like it was made for it, and the blankets are exactly the perfect weight so I can snuggle down and not overheat.

"You staying up for a while?" I ask. Sometimes I hear him bumping around the condo in the middle of the night. I packed a mask in case he wanted to stay up late here, so the light wouldn't bother me, but of course, that mask is in my missing suitcase.

"No. I'm ready," Gordo says. I doze as he pads across the room, then goes to the bathroom. He turns out the lights as he comes back, and the bed is so massive that the mattress on my side hardly even moves as I feel him pull back the covers. He grunts a few times as he rolls and gets comfortable, and then the space goes silent.

Really silent. I wonder if they use white noise or something to help block out the bustle of the Strip below.

I don't know why, but I slide my hand across the mattress. I truly do expect to find Gordo eventually, but I don't. I swing my palm over the buttery soft sheets, but there's no sign of him.

Until thick fingers brush my own. I gasp, surprised at the contact, and pull back.

"Just wanted to make sure you were there," Gordo says, like nothing weird has happened at all.

And it's not weird, is it? We're two guys in bed together. People need to sleep. No reason it can't be together. We both know what the ground rules are.

"Bailey?"

My heart is pounding. "Yeah?"

"You know my name isn't Gordon, right?"

I . . . did not know that. He signed a lease agreement when he moved in, and either I didn't notice what name he wrote on it, or I glossed over and assumed it was Gordon.

"Sure," I say.

"Gordo was my grandfather's name. I'm named after him."

I have to smother a laugh into my fluffy pillow. I cannot imagine a Grandpa named Gordo. I say, "Well, we all have to pretend to be someone we aren't this weekend."

He gets quiet for a minute. Then he says, "That's true, I guess."

I find his hand again and pat his fingers. "Goodnight, Gordo."

He lets out a sleepy yawn. "Goodnight, Bailey."

My last thought as I drift off is, I hope he doesn't snore.

5

———

ordo snores like a band saw. I'm not one for heavy machinery, but I'm pretty sure I should be wearing ear protection for noises this loud.

The room is fully dark, and I lie there waiting for him to stop, but he doesn't.

"Gordo," I say softly.

If the bed were any smaller, I'd be vibrating, and not in a good way.

"Gordo," I say it louder. The snoring stops. I relax. Gordo lets out a long exhale.

And then the world's most annoying wind orchestra picks up all over again.

"Gordo." I squirm across the expanse of the mattress until I find his shoulder. I shove at it. "Gordo, stop."

Maybe he's part dragon. That would explain why he and Bernard get along so well. Maybe his affinity for all those scaly things we live with is because of a lost heritage where his great-great-great-grandmother was a Viking princess kidnapped and added to some monster's hoard before they gently fell in love with each other and made little Gordos with wings and bushy eyebrows that snore through their massive nostrils and—

"Gordo." I press right up against him and shove him as hard as I can. He snorts, starts, mutters something like, "Just a minute," and then he rolls over.

Toward me.

He wraps me up in his enormous arms and spins me around like a top before he pulls me into his chest. His chin rests gently on the crown of my head, and he says, "Go to sleep, Bailey. It's not morning yet."

I smother a giggle. He smacks his lips. At least the snoring has stopped. It's kind of nice here. Feels like being loved up by a giant teddy bear. Gordo also has his shirt off and he is perfectly hairy. Exactly the right amount of chest hair to keep him—and a partner—warm at night.

But I can't stay. It wouldn't be fair. And yeah, I am a champion snuggler, so normally I don't mind spooning, but not when it feels like taking advantage of my best friend because he's too asleep to know what's going on.

Also—is that . . .

"Oh my God."

I shift a little bit, and Gordo sighs happily in his sleep as he presses a quickly growing erection against my ass.

"Oh no."

"Shh," he says. "We don't have to feed the tarantulas until the sun comes up."

Tarantulas? Has he been keeping fucking spiders at our place without telling me?

But I can't contemplate the question for too long because Jesus Christ he's huge. And now I'm getting hard too because I never met a dick I didn't like, and this is all wrong wrong wrong. Gordo's here to be my boyfriend. My very platonic boyfriend. We are not friends with benefits. He's not even into guys. And even if he were, I wouldn't take him to Vegas so I could fuck him —or let's be honest, so he could fuck me. We'd figure it out at home.

Desperately, I squirm, but his arms are a vice. Finally, I have to shimmy downward, letting the outline of his cock drag along my spine in a way that is far too distracting, until I've escaped the circle of his embrace and hit the end of the bed. I kick at the blankets until they pull free of the mattress and I tumble onto the floor where I sit, gasping and listening as Gordo's snoring resumes, at least more gently this time.

Jesus, did that just happen?

Totally involuntary though, right? He had no idea. Everyone gets a hard-on in their sleep now and then, right? He must have been dreaming—about spiders, apparently—but Vegas is built for sex. It's in the air. He could be dreaming about topless dancers in a chorus line for all I know.

I, for example, am dreaming about Gordo's dick.

And I'm very much awake.

My hand drifts down to my crotch, and it's like lightning. I have to bite back a whimper as I explore.

Fuck, this feels good.

I can't get back into bed. The bulge in my briefs is getting painful, and no matter how damn big that bed is, I can't very well jerk off next to him, regardless of how deeply asleep he is.

But as I sit on the floor and wait for it to go down, my brain transforms the soft sound of his snoring into gentle grunts that he'd make as he bent me over and shoved his gigantic—

Jesus, stop.

I've never fantasized about Gordo. Okay, maybe once the first time we met, but who wouldn't? If you're into beefy giants, Gordo is the poster boy. And yes, I may be compensating for my own height and thwarted aspirations of reaching that six-foot goal line, but I've never once acted on anything like that when it comes to Gordo.

But what happens in Vegas stays in Vegas, right?

Slowly, I crawl toward the bathroom, being careful not to make too much noise as I shut the door. I fumble until I find the lights, nearly blinding myself when I flick the big overhead one on, before shutting it quickly. The mirror over the sink has a few softer bulbs that I tell myself are perfect for mood lighting.

I stare at my reflection for a long time. Am I actually doing this? A cold shower would work almost as well, and then I could climb back into bed and Gordo would be none the wiser, and I'd still be able to look him in the eye in the morning.

But I want this. It doesn't have to be Gordo. Any big guy from my carefully inventoried and catalogued spank bank will do. Doesn't need to be weird. Can simply be about stress relief. Lord knows I've been under enough pressure lately.

But as I pull my underwear down and grip myself, the face I picture has red hair, soft lips, and a kind smile. It says, "Come on, Bailey," and it's the way Gordo says my name, and I can't help it.

"Oh God." It feels so good when I start to stroke. I squeeze my eyes shut because I've never liked watching myself jerk off. Seriously, it may feel amazing, but jackhammering on your penis is never glamorous. I lick my lips and imagine getting down on my knees, offering my mouth to Gordo.

Maybe he'd let me. Even straight guys appreciate a blow job.

No. Can't think about that. Can't think about what's possible, because then I'll make it awkward tomorrow.

So I go back to the previous image. We're naked. He's behind me. He says things like "You've got such a pretty ass" as he bends me forward, because Gordo would never say something like that, so that makes it okay for me to think it. I brace one elbow against the counter. I picture his hands on my ass. Maybe his mouth. Straight guys may appreciate a blow job, but rimming seems farther out of the realm of possibility for many. I imagine his tongue on my hole, wet and strong. Then his fingers. Blunt, wider than most, but so necessary for what's to come.

In case it's not clear, I'm what's to come. Very soon.

I'm breathing hard. My thighs are shaking. I think about what he felt like, pressed up against me in bed. What he'd feel like, stretching me open.

I only have a second to imagine the burn before my dick shoots off unexpectedly. I bite my lip to keep from shouting. He can't hear. This is so inappropriate. Friends. That's all we are, and we're good friends. I can't ruin it because I'm stressed and exhausted and horny.

But God, it feels good. I ride out the shockwaves and the spasms and wonder if Gordo makes any noise when he comes and then tell myself I don't get to wonder that because I've already crossed a line.

I clean up and fumble my way back to bed, making sure to keep the lights out. Gordo's still snoring softly. Slowly—so very slowly—I slide in next to him. Well, sort of next to him. There's no one between us, so we're technically next to each other. But I roll to face away from him and basically cling to the edge of the giant mattress like a life raft so as to put as much space between us as humanly possible.

I nearly jump out of my skin when Gordo says, "You okay?"

I definitely have to wait until my heart gets out of my throat before I can answer. "Yeah fine. Getting a drink of water. It's dry in here. Desert. You know."

My pulse pounds while I wait for him to say something else. Anything. "You took a long time," or "Why didn't you get me a drink too?" or "Sure didn't sound like you were getting water. It sounded like you were getting off."

But he remains blessedly silent.

I will live to wank another day. But not about Gordo. That can never happen again.

Just as I'm about to relax and accept that he really is asleep, he says, "Piña Colada, you're the prettiest girl."

That's good enough for me.

6

———

I wake up relaxed and refreshed in a way I haven't in weeks or possibly even months. Then I remember my hand on my dick and Gordo's name on my tongue and shame creeps in like a hangover.

Fuck.

I roll, and he's got his back to me, and that's a relief at least.

Except we're supposed to be having breakfast with Jake and Elias this morning.

Double fuck.

And I still have no clean clothes.

Triple—well, you get the idea.

Reluctantly, I drag myself out of bed. My stomach growls. I haven't had anything to eat since the plane last night. They served salmon with this orzo salad that was awesome, but it came in teeny-weeny-sized airplane servings, and so now I am a very hungry hippo.

At least if we meet up with Jake and Elias, there will be food.

The shower is heavenly. I wonder if Gordo would be opposed to getting one of these rainfall showerheads at our place. Of course, that question leads to me wondering what

Gordo looks like in the shower, and I promised myself that my extra-curricular activities last night were a one-night-only deal, so no, we won't be talking about showers any time soon.

I feel slightly more human as I get dried off. Putting my clothes back on doesn't sound fun, but at least I came from work yesterday, so what I have is appropriate to wear for the first day of the retreat.

Gordo, though . . .

I come out of the bathroom and he's over at the suite's little coffee station, trying to pour an espresso into the smallest paper cup I have ever seen.

He's also back in his Value Village chic look from yesterday.

"Is that what you're wearing?"

The question rips itself out of my mouth before I can stop it. It sounds judgey and I don't mean it to. Normally, I don't care what Gordo wears. He is very much his own man, and the various geckos, turtles, axolotls, and snakes that he's saved over his lifetime are definitely indifferent to his wardrobe choices.

He runs a hand down the front of his ancient T-shirt. "Yeah."

In for a penny . . . "Did you pack literally anything else?"

He glances at the rhinestone bag. "My bathing suit."

I can't help myself. My post-orgasm bliss evaporates in the face of the knowledge that Gordo, poor, kind, sweet Gordo, has packed literally nothing appropriate to wear on a three-day corporate event.

"We're supposed to be having breakfast with Jake and—"

"Jake the Jerk," he says, laughing softly to himself.

"Yes, Jake the Jerk. And Emu Elias. We're invited to breakfast with them in fifteen minutes, and you're telling me you didn't even pack a pair of pants? What about dinner? What about meeting my boss?"

He shrugs. "We're on vacation."

"It's a working vacation, Gordo." I bury my fingers in my hair as I pace the room.

"Well, I can buy something."

"You're going to have to. There are expectations. This is a corporate retreat."

Gordo lifts his tiny coffee to his lips and blows over the top. He takes a sip and says, "I'm not a very corporate kind of guy."

"You're also not my boyfriend," I say. "But I thought you could play along and follow simple instructions for a few days."

His face scrunches up. "You didn't say anything about what I was supposed to wear."

"I didn't think I had to."

Gordo looks positively devastated. "I'm sorry, Bailey."

Breakfast is clearly off the table. I am being an ass and I don't know how to stop. I don't have the bandwidth to be Gordo's babysitter while we're here, not on top of everything else.

I sigh. "I have to go to the first session. You'll be okay today? There's the casinos. A few weird-ass museums. I'll be back later this afternoon, and we can hang out, okay?"

He nods. He looks like he's going to crawl back into bed and hide from the world all day.

"I'm sorry," I say. "I shouldn't have snapped."

"I'll find some better clothes," he says.

"It doesn't matter. Be yourself. I shouldn't care what you wear."

He watches me carefully before he says, "But Jake the Jerk will care."

I think of Emu Elias in his skinny pants and polished loafers. He's exactly the kind of guy I'd picture Jake with.

"Yes, Jake will care."

Gordo nods, then he crosses the room and folds me into a big hug. I'm surprised by how much I need the contact. I should feel awkward after last night and about the fit I just threw, but instead I bury my nose into his chest and breathe in the cotton scent of him.

"I'll do better this afternoon," he says.

Oh, there it is. Now I feel like shit. But we can stand here all day and apologize some more, or we can move on. I give him one more squeeze and head off to my meetings.

Which are a disaster. They start with Jake getting in front of me as I walk into the kick-off speech from our new CEO.

"I thought we were having breakfast."

I make up a lie about Gordo and I sleeping in. He looks like he's going to push the issue, but the talk gets called to order.

Next are ice breakers. I hate ice breakers. I already know the people I work with. I have no desire to get to know the guys from the other company. They're all like Jake by the looks of it. Slick hair, custom suits. They high five each other whenever their region or a specific campaign gets mentioned.

I yawn.

Jake says, "Your big man wear you out?"

Why is he even sitting next to me? Shouldn't he be sitting with the other bigwigs down in front?

I glare at him. Without our partners here to keep up appearances, I don't have to be any nicer to him than I am at the office. He grins like he knows he's getting under my skin.

From there, it's an endless onslaught of meetings and talks about where we're headed, how we're going to get there, and why our new and improved benefits package means I can afford all the treatment I'll need for my bleeding ulcers when the fiscal year is over.

I want to crawl into bed and sleep for a million years.

But when I get back to the room, Gordo's waiting for me. He's still in the clothes from this morning. I make a point of not asking him about them.

Mercifully, my luggage is there too.

"Oh, thank God." I caress it like I've been reunited with a lost child after a shipwreck.

"Come on, Bailey." Gordo's practically hopping from foot to foot. "Let's go to the pool. It's time!"

I lug my suitcase onto the bed and open it up, checking for damage or missing items. "Time for what?"

When he doesn't answer, I check over my shoulder. He's got a massive grin on.

Fine. Whatever. He's excited and I was a dick to him this morning, so if he wants to hang out by the pool, we will. I find my trunks and try not to be shy when I get out of my work clothes while Gordo's in the room. We've seen each other naked before. It's inevitable when you live together. But it's always quick glimpses before someone closes a door or darts into a bedroom. I've never undressed in front of him.

But maybe I'm feeling weird about it because of last night.

The pool is typical Vegas. Sprawling, perfect aqua, with an army's worth of loungers and umbrellas around it.

I head straight for the two closest to us, but Gordo grabs my hand and pulls me toward the far side of the pool deck.

"This way," he says.

"What was wrong with those ones?"

He doesn't answer. He gets like this sometimes. Gordo's not great at words. He's good at ideas, but there's some kind of traffic jam between his brain and his mouth, and the words don't always come out. I've found it's easier to follow along. Often, whatever he's got in store is pretty cool. And really, if he wants to pick our pool loungers, I'm fine with that.

When we get to the other side, he spends a long time standing facing the hotel. It's a giant tower of glass, with the pool nestled in the curve of its concave facade. Gordo's looking up and squinting, but when I go to sit down, he puts a hand on my shoulder and gently pushes me, so I'm one lounger over. He squints some more. Pushes me one more step to the right.

"Okay," he says with a smile and settles onto a chair.

"What was that about?" I ask as I spread out a towel.

He grins. "There's a death ray."

I nearly leap back to my feet. "A what?"

He tries to explain. Something about the curve of the hotel and the angle of the sun and how the online reviews mention things like melted drink glasses and scorched towels.

"And we're sitting here why?" I say.

"Because it's so cool." He's ordered a ginger ale and an extra cup of ice, which he's placed on the little table between us and keeps moving from one position to another while he squints up at the gleaming building above us.

Honestly, most of Gordo's ideas are good, or entertaining at least, but I'm not real comfortable with the idea that the hotel might incinerate us at any moment.

But as I'm about to suggest we leave the cup of ice to its fate and find somewhere shadier, a voice goes, "Well look who it is," and my unease gets redirected.

Coming toward us are Jake and Elias. Dammit. I thought we were safe until dinner. Jake's in slim-fit Hawaiian print board shorts and a pair of obviously designer sunglasses, and Elias is wearing a gauzy purple caftan and gold flip flops. Between Jake's perfectly sculpted chest and Elias's swooshy . . . well . . . everything, they're hard to look away from.

"Oh, hi," I say, and Gordo waves a hand at them.

"How's the water?" Jake says with a big smile.

"We haven't been in yet," I say.

"We're waiting for the death ray," Gordo says, flashing big square teeth.

"The what?" Elias looks nervous. I can't decide if that's a good thing or a bad thing. On the one hand, maybe it'll convince

Elias that they need to find seats somewhere else. On the other hand, if Gordo upsets him, I'm sure to hear about it from Jake later.

Gordo explains. Elias looks anxious. Jake looks bored. A poolside server overhears us and stops long enough to reassure Elias that the hotel has a specific reflective coating that means the death ray isn't actually a thing, and then he takes another round of drink orders. Elias seems relieved as the server departs. Gordo's annoyed. He dumps the half-melted ice cubes into his ginger ale.

"So, Gordon," Elias asks as he reclines in the lounger next to him, "what did you get up to today while our menfolk were busy being important?"

"I wandered around. Went shopping. Had a manicure."

The last one brings me up short. Gordo both is and is not exactly the kind of man I would expect to enjoy a little pampering, but I struggle to picture him wandering into one of the lavish hotel spas here and asking for a treatment.

"Did you have a hard time getting away from the office to come for the long weekend?" Jake asks.

Gordo shakes his head. "Not really."

"Which division of Rolls-Royce do you work for? I know a couple people who were there for a while after a merger."

Gordo's face clouds and my stomach drops all the way to my knees. Oh shit. I forgot about that little lie.

I glance at Jake, and he may be speaking to Gordo, but he's watching me. That jackass. He knows. He knows I was lying through my teeth, and now he's waiting to catch me out on it.

"Well actually," I say, even though I have no idea how to finish that sentence.

"Actually," Gordo says, "I've been functioning in more of a consultant role at Rolls for the last six months or so."

What?

"Oh really?" Jake leans in, still fishing for opportunity.

"Yes." Gordo smiles blandly, like he tells people about this all the time. "They bought my patent but asked me to stay on while they finish the design on the new engine controls. I should be done by the end of the year."

Staring is rude, but what the hell else am I supposed to do? That's more than I've ever heard Gordo speak in a single go, and somehow he knows what I told Jake.

My mouth is open, so to hide my shock I say, "I'm going for a swim. Do you want to come?"

Gordo smiles up at me. "Sounds perfect."

I hastily strip out of my T-shirt, ignoring the look Jake is giving me. Elias is either asleep on his lounger or pretending we don't exist. I can't tell behind his sunglasses, and I don't actually care.

What I do care about is Gordo, who is currently . . .

Oh, holy Hannah.

He was still in his old shorts when we came down, and I guess I thought he was going to swim in those. Instead, he pulls them down and neatly folds them on his chair before he grabs his T-shirt and tugs it off over his head and—

Oh my God.

"Is that . . ." I have to swallow and try again. "Is that bathing suit new?"

On Gordo's other side, Elias makes a small squeaking noise that means he's not asleep after all, and he's seeing what I'm seeing and—

Gordo is a mountain of a man in the smallest, best-fitting swim trunks I've ever seen.

"These?" he asks, brushing his hands over the blue and navy material. "No, I've had these for ages."

He is . . . He is the bear-rug equivalent of a male pin-up. The mid-century so-called "athletic models" who every little gay boy pretended to get into fitness for, when in fact they wanted to see pictures of arms and pecs and abs and thighs . . .

Holy shit his thighs.

Gordo. My ultra-casual, thrift-store-shopping, bearded-dragon-saving roommate is . . .

He's a beefcake.

Like he knows what I'm thinking, he turns to say something to Elias, which only succeeds in giving me a glimpse of the way his barely-there trunks are framing his perfect ass. Jesus, you could crack a walnut and—

I'm in the pool so fast I don't even have time to think about how deep it is . . . or isn't. My feet hit the bottom faster than I expect, and I more or less collapse in on myself while pain radiates over my knees. I swallow a mouthful of chlorinated pool water and come up spluttering in time to see Gordo casually stroll down the stairs that aren't more than fifteen feet from where I went in. Horrified heat rolls up my skin as the water laps at his legs, then wicks up his tiny trunks, making them cling to him and—

Oh my God.

I'm hot for Gordo.

7

———

I have a problem. And while the solution to many problems is more cowbells—or is that the solution to more fevers?—it will not solve mine. Certainly, though, the image of Gordo wandering around the pool deck and chatting with Emu Elias while he shows off his body to the world like a male Bond Girl—Bond Boy? Bond Man? Is he just James Bond at that point?—is going to clang inside my head with the musicality of a rusty old bell for days.

And it gets worse.

We ride the elevator back up to our room. Gordo stands silently beside me. He's got his T-shirt over his shoulder and his shorts folded over one arm. If I didn't know better, I'd swear he's doing his best to torment me. His chest is a matt of red hair and I want to thread my fingers through it. I want to see if he's sensitive at the spot where his beard meets his ear. I want to do so many things to him and beg him to do so many things to me, and it's all so very wrong.

I can't be crushing on Gordo. That wasn't part of the deal. And what would we do when we go home? Not like I can moon about the condo quietly pining and drawing *Bailey + Gordo =*

LUV in steam on the bathroom mirror. Gordo's pretty unphased by the world around him, but even he'd be bound to notice one of these days.

I need to get laid. That's the solution. It's been a while, and last night was inexcusable. Clearly the hormones have gone to my brain and are short-circuiting my usual decision-making processes.

After the pool, I take an extra-long time in the shower, trying to sweat the feelings out through my pores. When I get back to Toronto, I'm going to find a guy online, enjoy a good hard dicking—ew, does anyone actually say that?—and everything else will return to normal. I can focus on surviving life with Jake the Jerk, and Gordo will never have to know.

But then I walk out into our suite, and all my excellent intentions come crashing down.

"Is that—" I choke on the words. I have to grip my towel so hard my knuckles turn white, but my fingers have gone numb and I'm not sure if I'll be able to hold the damn thing up otherwise. "So you do have a suit?"

Gordo turns fully toward me, smoothing a hand down his front, over the perfectly fitted suit jacket he's wearing, along with pants to match, a black shirt with the finest white polka dots, and a single line of white where a pocket square peeks out from his breast pocket.

"Does it look okay?" His question is so earnest, I can't stop myself when I giggle, but then his eyes go wide and I have to hold my hand out to let him know I have more to say.

"It looks great." Jesus, it's more than great. He's done something to his hair too, and the shag has turned into a sophisticated curl, almost like a modern pompadour.

He grins. "Does it? The woman said it fit well."

I blink. "What woman?"

He unbuttons the jacket but holds onto the fronts. "I went to one of the stores across from the hotel. The woman who helped me was so nice. But are you sure?" He turns and glances over his shoulder. Unfortunately for me, his grip on the material means it's pulled taut across the back, giving me a perfectly double-vented view of his ass in pants that are . . .

"It's fine." My smile hurts.

He turns back, so at least I can breathe again. He looks appeased. "She said normally they would tailor the clothes for someone my size, but since I needed them tonight, they wouldn't have time, and anyway, she said it was pretty close, so—"

"Wait. Wait." I take a step back. "Are you telling me you bought this today?"

He shrugs. "I told you I went shopping."

"But you bought—" I gesture at his clothes, then gulp as I catch a glimpse of the label inside the jacket as he does the buttons up again. Jesus. I've never been able to afford that, no matter how much BGS&M pays me in bonuses and incentives. "That must have cost a fortune."

"I wanted to look good, and they didn't have a lot in my size. You were right about my clothes. I couldn't go to dinner dressed the way I was."

And now I feel like shit. I shouldn't have given him a hard time this morning. I was pissed at myself for the whole top-secret midnight masturbation thing, but that's not Gordo's fault. None of this is. He's bending over backwards to be here for me, and I've treated him like a jerk.

I take a deep breath. "Thank you."

His smile is soft. "For what?"

"For coming with me. For playing along. For the clothes. You didn't have to do that."

He gives me an up and down look that would normally get

my blood stirring again, but I've resolved to be good. He says, "Is that what you're wearing?"

My cheeks heat for an entirely different reason as I tighten the towel around my hips. "No."

He nods like that's what he was expecting. "You get dressed. I'm going to go watch the fountains again."

Unfortunately, even Gordo watching the fountains is distracting, to say the least. He's backlit, and as I hop on one foot, trying to pull a sock on, I can't take my eyes off his silhouette against the dancing lights of the Strip.

I'm so screwed. How is it possible that a guy I have been living with for close to two years is suddenly the object of every fantasy in my head? I have sales targets to hit, a jackass boss to avoid, and all I want to do is mess up Gordo's hair and strip his designer suit from his skin inch by inch.

By the time we get to dinner, I'm so strung out I'm practically vibrating. The VPs—and their plus-ones—are all meeting at this Italianate restaurant that's meant to look like we've all come to accept an offer we can't refuse. I love Vegas. It's so ostentatiously tacky. But right now, with Gordo at my shoulder, I can't even enjoy it.

Of course, the first people we see are Jake and Elias. They're talking with Lachlan, who looks unhappy to have been cornered.

"Come on," I say as I put a palm in the middle of Gordo's back to guide him. The gesture feels awkward, but if we were really together, this is something I would do, isn't it? Touch him, without feeling unsure, or that every eye in the room is on me?

For Gordo's part, he doesn't seem to care. He doesn't lean into my hand, but he doesn't move away either. I do my best to smile as we approach Lachlan and the others.

"Hey, guys!" I nearly say, "fancy meeting you here," but this dinner is literally a planned retreat event, and also sounds too much like something Jake would say. So instead I go with, "Lachlan, you know Gordon, my . . . um . . . partner?"

Sure. Why not up the ante? Two days ago we were roommates. Yesterday we were boyfriends. Now I'm just grateful my suit jacket covers the perpetual half-chub I'm sporting, so why the hell shouldn't we be partners? I can propose to him at the top of the fake Eiffel Tower across the street tomorrow.

Lachlan looks surprised as he takes in the two of us. Gordo says, "It's nice to see you again," like he's used to making small talk at these corporate cocktail parties. Lachlan shakes his hand, but his gaze is on me, and if he outs me right now, I'll murder him. The blood on the terrazzo floor will match the mafia ambience perfectly.

He says, "How was your afternoon?" and we chit chat about pools and poker for a bit. Gordo says something about the death ray, which makes Elias jumpy again, and I have to bite my lip at the renewed disappointment on Gordo's face when no one seems as fascinated with the physics of it all as he is.

I say, "Don't worry, babe. We'll go see the horses, and you can tell me everything you know about the wild mustangs."

"Horses?" Elias leans in. "What horses?"

I'm still trying to figure out if I liked the way "babe" felt on my tongue, so I don't answer, but it doesn't matter because Gordo launches into a whole monologue about mustangs and the Bureau of Land Management and the mythos of the American frontier. Elias looks rapt, and I'm annoyed that they seem to have something in common.

Jake must be too because he lifts up his empty glass and says, "I'm going to the bar. Bailey, Lachlan, we're sitting together at dinner."

He very definitely doesn't use any question marks in that sentence. Lachlan and I both give matching smiles of false enthusiasm as Jake makes his way through the crowd. Gordo and Elias are chattering a mile a minute about horse racing in the Mongolian desert, and I honestly don't understand half of what they're saying.

I put a gentle hand on Gordo's arm. "Do you want something to drink?"

He smiles at me and says, "Sure," before he goes right back to talking with Elias.

Somehow, being dismissed by the man only pretending to be my boyfriend hurts more than I expect.

Lachlan and I head toward the bar—being careful to give Jake a wide berth—and when we're far enough away, he takes hold of my elbow and pulls me into a corner where a small stone child pees gracefully into a fountain.

"What the hell?" I say, dodging the spray.

Lachlan's eyes are huge. He says, "Isn't that your roommate?"

"Shh!" I wave at him. "Keep it down."

"You're dating your roommate?"

I glare. Lachlan's been under a lot of pressure lately, which is the only reason I give him any kind of pass. I say, "For the purposes of this weekend, yes. We're dating."

"Finally."

I stumble back from the shock and the cherub rocks ominously, splattering my sleeve.

"Excuse me?"

"I mean, he's basically the only person you talk about."

I glower. "Because I work too hard to have friends besides you."

But Lachlan keeps talking like I haven't said anything. "You're always going on about his baking and his pets. Didn't he make cricket cupcakes once? I thought you said he was straight."

"He is!" My brain is reeling at the thought of insect cupcakes.

"He's a lot better looking than you told me he was."

"Hey!" I'm suddenly outraged on Gordo's behalf. Also, when

did I ever say he wasn't good looking? His fashion sense is unconventional, but he's got a great smile and big hands and a chest you can—

Ugh. Damn. Now I'm thinking about Gordo's body again.

"Well, I wouldn't say he's unattractive," I say carefully.

Lachlan shakes his head incredulously. "But you're always talking about him like he's some kind of stoner Betty Crocker who hangs around your condo all day."

I try to make my shrug charming as I wheel Lachlan back around to the bar. "Turns out Gordon cleans up good."

Lachlan's still staring, even as we move forward. "Is he wearing a Redhill suit?"

"Trigani," I say. "Bought it this morning."

"Remind me what he does for a living?"

"He makes rocket engines at Rolls-Royce," I say, because the best way to get through this weekend is to stick to at least one lie.

But I'm starting to wonder about Gordo's real job myself. Something doesn't add up, and it's not only the way the suit fits him. It's how he looks totally comfortable as I hand him a dry martini, while he talks with Jake and Elias, and doesn't bat an eyelash when Ed Morton, CEO for all of BGS&M, comes over to say hi. I've never met the man and he cuts an intimidating figure, but Gordo keeps on talking like he's used to this kind of glad-handing and folds Ed right into the conversation. I can hardly get him to string ten words together when we're alone at home, but here, he's the life of the party.

"Bailey," he says excitedly as we sit down for dinner. "Elias invited us to come see the emus this summer. Doesn't that sound like fun?"

And yet, there is the roommate I know and lo— Shit, no. Somehow that word makes my brain go all staticky. I accidentally knock one of the six knives set next to my plate to the floor with a clatter.

"Sounds amazing," I say weakly.

Spending another weekend with Jake and Elias sounds like torture.

Hell, spending tonight with them is torture. Jake slides into the open seat next to mine.

"Hey team," he says with a toothy grin. "What's on the menu?"

My skin crawls. I would shy away from him, but it would be A) obvious and B) force me closer to Gordo, and if I touch him again, I may decide to crawl into his lap and beg him to C) save me, D) kiss me, or E) take me right there on the table.

I'm so screwed.

8

———

Dinner is . . .

Whatever Gordo wants, I'm going to pay him back tenfold when we get home. No one should have to sit through this for free. Dinner is about what you'd expect. Jake dominates the conversation and also drinks a bottle and a half of wine while he does it. Lachlan is so stressed out that he follows along and proceeds to get absolutely wasted.

"Do you like cheese?" he asks me at one point.

"Sure?"

"I used to work for a place that sold cheese. Best job I ever had." He jabs a finger at me. "We should sell more cheese, Bailey. What do you say?"

"I like cheese," Gordo, sitting between us, says. "I'm part of a co-op that owns Jersey cows. They make amazing cheese."

I glare at him. "Where's my cheese? We never have cheese at home."

He smiles affectionately at me. "You're lactose intolerant."

Right. I poke at my dessert, apple pie while everyone around me got cheesecake. "Thanks for reminding me."

Gordo pats my hand and takes a bite of his cheesecake,

leaving the fork between his lips as he obviously savours it. I wonder what he likes. Does he prefer cheesecake or pie? Chocolate or vanilla? We don't eat any more elaborate than ramen noodles and takeout. I work too late to cook, and my breakfast routine consists of coffee until I'm on the verge of a migraine.

Lachlan laughs. "You two are good together. Bailey needs someone looking out for him. I admit, I always thought you were straight, Gor—"

"Okay!" I push up to my feet. "Time to call it a night."

Gordo glances mournfully at his last bite of cheesecake, still on his plate, but he rises too. Unfortunately, Jake, on my other side, joins us, using my sleeve to help pull himself up. "A night? What are you talking about? We're just getting started!"

"Yeah!" Lachlan agrees, bobbing in his seat with bleary eyes. "Just getting started."

"No." I pull my jacket off the back of my chair. "Sorry. Jetlag. You know."

"Bailey." He may be tipsy, but even so, Jake's voice goes ice cold. "It's not time to go yet. We're still working on our team building."

I shudder. I know that tone. He used it so often when we were kids. *"No, we're okay. We were only playing. Weren't we, Bailey?"* And I knew that if I didn't play along, he'd make my life the next day ten times worse, so I smiled and waved and pretended that having another boy grinding my face into the mud was part of having fun. Bonding. Boys will be boys.

I'm so fucking tired of team building. So tired of trying to get along. I glance at Gordo, and he's watching me with that direct gaze that always makes me more confident in who I am and my own decision making. We should go back to the hotel room and crash.

But Lachlan's on the other side of him . . . or on top of him, really. He's smiling and looks like he's so excited to be there and he says, "Come, Bailey. Let's go." And when I glance back at Jake, his attention has turned from me to Lachlan too, and his eyes narrow and my stomach tightens. Because Jake is sizing up Lachlan the way a python eyes a microwaved mouse, and Lachlan is pretty much as defenceless. He's got one arm around Gordo's shoulders, but his smile is as blurry as his eyes.

I can't leave him.

I glance again at Gordo. He's watching me, waiting for my cue. In his suit and his slicked-back hair, he looks ready for battle.

Fuck it. We're going in.

"Okay!" I say, giving Jake my best grin. "Let's get the party started."

As it turns out, Jake's had things planned for a while. We all —Gordo and me, Jake and Elias, Lachlan, and a few other guys and their spouses—pile into a few Ubers and drive up the Strip. Jake has a booth booked at a rooftop club. It's dark, with atmospheric lighting that casts long shadows, and go-go dancers—both men and women on tall pedestals lit from above—who dance to raging electronica with a thumping bass. The staff treat us like high rollers, and Jake makes a big show about ushering people behind the rope that sections off where we're sitting from the writhing masses on the dance floor and crammed up against the bar. Bottles are brought to the table, drinks are poured. Then more. Then some kind of electric green shot for good measure.

"To the team!" Jake lifts his glass high in the air. Lachlan follows suit, just as loud and proud. Elias sits quietly next to Jake but is doing his darnedest to keep up on the booze front.

Beside me, Gordo has hardly touched his drinks.

I lean into him, nose right above his ear. "You okay?"

He nods. "Are you?"

I'm tired. And stressed. And now I feel like I need to be on high alert because Jake's got something up his sleeve, and I have to be ready for it.

Without thinking, I drop my forehead to Gordo's shoulder. Since it's about the width of an ironing board, there's lots of room for me to rest there. More still when he puts an arm around me and tugs me closer.

"Should we go?" he asks.

I shake my head but don't sit up. It's warm here. Safe. A few hours ago, the idea of being this close to Gordo would have been torture, but now it's the only place I want to be, even if I have to plaster myself to the fabric of his designer shirt all night. Because Gordo is somehow beyond all this bullshit, and I'm to blame for dragging him into it.

As if to prove my point, Jake points an accusatory finger at us. "No!" He leers like a frat boy. "None of that."

I roll my eyes. "You of all people can't give me a hard time for snuggling with my boyfriend."

Gordo's hand tightens slightly on my arm at the word, and I'm sorry for putting him in this position. It was too much to ask.

But Jake's still waving his finger in our direction. "No napping. Wake up! It's time to dance!"

"Yeah!" Lachlan crows behind him, booze splashing over the rim of his glass, even if he doesn't seem to notice. "Let's dance."

They make their way past the velvet rope. I try to say no, but Lachlan basically wrenches me to my feet and drags me behind him, laughing as he goes. He's wasted, and when we finally get to the dancefloor, he's not dancing so much as walking a wobbly path around our group, then expanding his trajectory to encompass other people. Most of them seem willing to tolerate the drunk guy in the suit as long as he keeps his hands to himself.

Well. We're out here. Might as well dance to Jake's tune. He and Elias are basically trying to swallow each other's faces as if they're back in high school. I turn away from them and find myself face to face with Gordo. He looms over me, so tall his face is half in shadow by the too-trendy lighting. If he's dancing, it's not much. More like he's keeping time like a heartbeat while people gyrate around him.

Wordlessly, he spins me so I face away from him. He keeps his hands on my hips, so we're both moving to the same rhythm. I pat his knuckles, letting him know what a good boyfriend he's being. I won't ask him for more. He's here. He got dressed up for me and he's playing the part, and that's enough.

His gaze is directed somewhere in front of us. I follow the line, and he's watching the female go-go dancer closest to the bar. She's everything you'd expect a dancer in a Vegas club to be. High heels, lots of sequins. She's got great breasts—even I can appreciate good proportions, even if they do nothing for me sexually—held up in a rhinestone bra. She winks at me when she catches my eye. I'd tell her I'm far more interested in the guy two pedestals over, who's dancing in combat boots and neon bootie shorts, but the truth is I'm not even very into him right now. Not when I've got Gordo's hands on me, even if his attention is elsewhere.

I turn again so I can pull his head down and speak into his ear over the music.

"She's pretty," I say.

His hand on the small of my back is like an iron.

"She's a good dancer," he says. "Good rhythm."

"You look great tonight," I say.

He smiles at me shyly. "Thank you."

"Mr. High Roller, turning heads. If I weren't here with you, there would be twenty women lined up to take you back to their rooms."

He laughs, making my body vibrate against his. Someone bumps into me and I'm pressed closer to him.

"Good thing I'm here with you then," he says. His hands

slide down to hold me tighter, and I am a masochist, because being this close to him, with all the other images that play over and over in my head, is torture. I want him to be here with me. Not pretend. Not some lie we made up so I could save face with my asshole boss. I want a guy like Gordo—no, not a guy like him, I want *Gordo*—to touch me like he is right now and know that it means more than a good friend keeping a promise.

I glance back at the dancer. She's still watching me and smiles when our eyes meet again. Does she know? Does she know how much I want the man who is watching her when I want his eyes on me? It's her job to be like this. Distantly flirty. Men buy into the fantasy all the time. She's here to make them think about the possibility. To make them drink more as they try to loosen up so they can take risks they never would at home. What happens in Vegas . . . and all that.

But what happens with me and Gordo won't stay in Vegas, because in a few days, we have to go home together. Go back to normal together.

I need space—maybe a whole night's worth—to get my head on straight.

I pull Gordo's head down so he'll be able to hear me clearly, even though I'm about to say perhaps the most asinine thing I have ever uttered in my whole life.

"If you wanted to hook up with someone tonight, that would be okay."

He jerks back, but I don't let go. "What?"

I stumble on because I need the confirmation of his red-blooded heterosexuality to remind me of why I can't have what I want and why I need to behave myself so I don't lose my room-mate and best friend when we get home.

"It's Vegas." I try for a roguish grin. "If you wanted to some-thing quick and casual, there's nowhere better. No judgement.

Go back to her room. It wouldn't be hard. I'm sorry for making you pretend to be someone you're not."

When he pulls back a second time, I let him go, and he half trips over his feet. His movements are so sudden he nearly runs over a woman in a skin-tight dress and has to take a minute to help her find her footing again and make sure she's okay. She smiles up at him with boozy stars in her eyes, and it's so clear how easy it would be. When Gordo puts on that gentle giant face, he's irresistible. Her friends are waiting a few steps away, but all her attention is on him. He could sweep her off her feet in every possible way and they'd be out of here in minutes.

Instead, he pats her shoulder and gently guides her toward her expectant entourage. They watch him and giggle as he turns back to me, but he doesn't make a move.

In fact, as he closes the space between us, he puts his hands on my shoulders and stares down at me. His eyes are only visible from time to time as the lights wheel around us, and I can't make out what he's thinking.

"That was a bad suggestion, wasn't it?" I say, feeling heat spreading up the back of my neck.

He frowns, bushy eyebrows creeping together. His mouth is pressed into a straight line. Even his neatly groomed beard—God, did he even get a beard trim today?—looks severe. He licks his lips and leans down so he's speaking directly into my ear.

He says, "Bailey. Are you under the impression that I'm straight?"

If he didn't have his hands on me, I would fall down. I have to grip his wrists to hold myself up. When he straightens again, his expression is all seriousness. A sharp crack of laughter escapes from me, but Gordo doesn't react. Doesn't laugh too, doesn't look shy. He's waiting for me to make the next move.

Eruditely, I say, "You're not?"

And, slowly, he shakes his head.

Holy shit.

I gape. "All this time?"

Gordo shrugs. "It's not exactly a new thing."

I exhale, letting this information settle, going back over the days, months, weeks—hell, the *years*—we've lived together and looking for the signs I missed.

There weren't any. I'm sure of it.

And now we're here, trapped performing for Jake the Jerk, and this all would have been so much easier if—

I slap at his chest. "Well, why the fuck didn't you tell me?"

Gordo looks baffled as he opens his mouth. "Bailey."

Except then Lachlan weaves his way toward us, fresh drink in his hand. "Hey, guys," he slurs. "How come you're not dancing?"

"Not now." I try to push him away, but he gets tangled up around my arm, clinging like a sock fresh from the dryer.

"Bailey," he says.

"Not now," I say again.

And then Lachlan barfs on my shoes.

9

———

I don't want to talk about it. Hell, I don't even want to think about it.

The next few moments are a lot of swirling lights and loud music, and Jake pointing and laughing and Lachlan looking mortified—and possibly puking again into an empty champagne bucket—and finally Gordo's hands on my shoulders drawing me away, and I'm too embarrassed and upset to lean into the comfort he's offering, so I shrug him off and stalk out of the club while my damp socks—

Ew.

No.

Not talking about it. Not even to Gordo. We ride the whole way back to the hotel silently. I'm so annoyed. Pissed off. Humiliated. Confused.

What does Gordo mean he's not straight? What does he mean he's never been straight? Not that I'd have jumped him the day he moved in, but we could have been different. Talked differently. We didn't necessarily have to be boyfriends, but we'd have been a different kind of friend.

As we enter the hotel, I toe out of my shoes. Socks go in the garbage can by the sliding front doors. Gordo offers a hand to help me balance while I take them off, but I use the wall instead. I ignore the strange looks as I cross the lobby barefoot.

As we ride the elevator, I feel like I might shatter into a thousand pieces and would probably be fine with that development.

Gordo says, "Why do you work with those people?"

I say, "I don't want to talk about it."

So we don't. We walk silently to our room, and I let us in, but I don't hold the door for Gordo. He's a big boy. He can manage. Instead, I dart for the bathroom, strip out of my pants, and climb into the shower to spray myself off from the ankles down.

"Are you okay?" Gordo asks from the hall.

"What do you think?" I foam up the bar of soap in my hands and scrub at my feet. I've pulled the hand nozzle off its holder, trying to manage the spray, since I'm still in my shirt and my underwear, but I don't succeed. The shirt sticks to my chest in wet dots as I step out of the shower and nearly break an ankle as I miss the bathmat and slip on the tile floor.

"Bailey?" Gordo bursts in as I'm flailing.

"Get out!"

This afternoon, when we came back from the pool, this kind of scenario would have been perfect. I slip in the bathroom and Gordo rushes in. Here I am, half out of my clothes, and there he is, all big caring concern. Oops. I fall into his arms. Shenanigans ensue.

Tonight though, I have too much rattling around in my head for sexy hijinks. Gordo must see some of it on my face because he slowly backs away and closes the bathroom door behind him as he retreats. In the end, I strip out of the rest of my ruined outfit and get back in the shower, letting the hot water roll over me until my world straightens again.

Except nothing's straight. At least not Gordo.

I put on one of the monogrammed hotel bathrobes and stare

at myself in the mirror for a long time. Twenty-four hours ago, I eyed myself up as I decided whether or not to indulge in clandestine masturbatory fantasies about a man who I thought could never want me as much as I wanted him in that moment. And now I find out that's maybe not true?

Except it still might be. Being not straight is not the same as being into a particular queer person. Not all vegetarians like tofu, not all pop music fans think Beyoncé had one of the best videos of all time, etc., etc. And he's never given even the slightest hint of any interest in the entire history of our acquaintance. His not-straightness does not conflate attraction to me.

I can't very well hide in the bathroom all night. I let myself out silently. The room is dark except for one lamp by the massive bed. Gordo's down in the living room, facing the fountain.

I could go to bed. Easy enough to slip under the covers and will this whole day—hell this whole trip—to be over.

But if nothing else, I should apologize to Gordo.

He's taken his jacket off, and when I come to stand next to him, his shirt sleeves are pushed up and he's got his bare forearms crossed over his chest. Ugh. Good forearms are my true weakness. I don't know why I never noticed his before since Gordo never met a T-shirt he didn't like. He's been flaunting his freckly fuzzy forearms around our condo on a daily basis and I was oblivious to their charms.

"Sorry," I say, stuffing my hands into the robe's oversized sleeves. "I get grouchy when there's vomit between my toes."

Gordo wrinkles his nose. "I thought we weren't talking about it."

We watch the fountain. It's honestly better than TV. We're so high up that there's a delay between the walls of water splashing down into the lagoon and the crash of the impact. I hope Gordo's enjoying it. It's the least I can do for him.

When it all goes dark, we stay watching the lights and the crush of humanity as it moves up and down the Strip.

Finally, when I'm about to crawl out of my skin if I don't ask him, I say, "So you're gay."

He's quiet for a long time. Long enough I think I've upset him. Finally, he says, "No, I've been with women too."

Fine by me. "So you're bi."

He turns away, but he only goes to the sectional before he sinks down, claiming the corner where the two halves of the sofa meet. He spreads his hairy bare forearms over the back of the leather, and I have to fight a shudder at the sight he makes, still imposing and impeccable, so very different from the Gordo I've known. Everything about him is different.

He says, "More like pan. Demi, actually. I don't care about the equipment. I care about the people."

Of course he does. Of course that's how he'd be. The answer is so perfectly Gordo it's obvious.

I sit at the far edge of the couch. "But what about Scarlett Johansson?"

Gordo laughs softly. "What about her?"

"She— You—" You know what? It doesn't matter. I read all the signals wrong. I'm going to have to watch the Avengers again and see what part of her character arc I missed. "Why didn't you tell me? About you."

Gordo reaches one long arm up until he finds the switch on the wall. He flicks it, and lights come on overhead, tucked behind panels that mean they warm the space, but aren't harsh. I pull the neck of my robe closer to me.

Gordo says, "It's complicated. Not everyone understands. When you tell them you're demisexual, people don't understand how that's different from committed monogamy, because of course you're attracted to people you're emotionally close to. But it's not really like that."

The appropriate thing to say here would be that I, at least, get it. But that wouldn't be true. As a teenager, as soon as I realized all the magical things an adult penis could do, I wanted to do them all, with anyone who was male and interested in doing them with me too. That's probably the exact opposite of what Gordo's talking about.

Gordo says, "I've only figured it out in the last couple years. For a long time, I was like you."

"A drama queen?" I say hopefully.

He laughs, and the small sound makes me feel a little better. "I worked too hard. Didn't have time for relationships, so it didn't matter that I wasn't with anyone. It was only when I stopped and had space for myself again that I realized I didn't feel the way most people do."

There's a lot to unpack there. "I can't imagine you working too hard at anything," I say. "Except maybe building a new terrarium. It doesn't have to be a spa, you know. Turtles are totally happy with a few rocks and a puddle."

Gordo smiles. "You think the turtles don't like my terrariums?"

I scoot a little closer to him as our conversation starts to feel familiar again. "I think you spoil the hell out of the turtles, Gordo."

"Animals are easy to take care of. People are a lot harder."

Especially when they don't have all the information. But I don't say that. He's never owed me any explanation.

I say, "So the whole time we've known each other, you've never been with someone else?"

He shakes his head. "No."

"Because you're demisexual?"

Gordo runs a hand through his hair, messing up the perfect style. I breathe easier as a bit of his shaggy persona comes back.

He says, "Because I wanted to be with you."

Oh. I laugh. Gordo, who I would never have credited with having any serious game when it comes to romance, he slid that one in there. "Very smooth." I grin.

But he looks uncomfortable. "When you said you wanted me to come this weekend, I thought you . . ." He trails off, dragging one finger along the stitching of the sofa.

My heart slams to a halt. "You thought it was real?"

He shrugs. "I thought. Maybe."

How many more times is my thoughtlessness going to leave me feeling like shit on this trip?

"I'm sorry. I didn't think—I saw Jake and I panicked. He saw your picture on my screensaver and he asked if we were together." As I've been speaking, I've been slowly making my way across the sofa, and now I'm on my knees next to him. I squeeze his thigh. "I'm sorry, Gordo. You're my best friend. No one else would do as much as you do for me."

He covers my hand with his. His mouth twitches, and he stares up at the ceiling. His rusty caterpillar eyebrows do a little dance. He says, "And if I wanted to not be a pretend boyfriend? If I wanted it to be real?"

Considering where things were at an hour ago, this evening has taken a delightful turn. I say, "We could work on that. Possibly. It doesn't have to be pretend. We could take it slow and—" I yelp as big hands settle around me and pull me forward, arranging me until I'm straddling Gordo's lap. I'm suddenly very aware of the fact that I'm wearing nothing underneath this robe as the fluffy material bunches up over Gordo's massive legs. "Or not," I say. "Slow is one option, but not the only choice. We can go as fast as you like."

Which, if the way his mouth surges to meet mine, is pretty darn fast. Gordo is an excellent kisser, as it turns out. His lips are firm and demanding; his beard is soft and tickles at my chin. I whimper when his tongue pushes into my mouth and more when his fingers slide under my robe, running up my thigh.

"Oh Jesus, Gordo." I groan as he kisses down my throat, forcing my head up. He's so big. Like a pillar of muscle. I can lean into him and let my whole body go slack, and he'll catch me. The only problem is, the more he touches me, the more he kisses me, the more I let myself get pulled into what he's offering, it's harder and harder to hide how . . . well . . . hard I'm getting, with only the fluff of the bathrobe to cover me.

"Gordo," I say, "what do you want to do tonight? How far do you want to go? Maybe I should put some clothes on if we're going to—"

But he drags my hand down between us and places it on his groin and—oh. Hello. Nice to see you again. I may already be wearing next to nothing, but Gordo's erection is doing its best to bust through the seams of his designer pants, and that seems like a waste of good money.

"Need a little help?" I say, cupping him through the fabric. He makes an entirely un-Gordo-like noise, growling as he thrusts into my grip, his eyes full of caveman heat. "You sure? We don't have to. We could just be boyfriends for a while. The benefits could happen—"

Once again, I'm manhandled—and oh my God, I think I'm going to love how this man handles me—until I'm lying down on the sofa with Gordo looming over me, braced on his arms. My robe has fallen open, and there's no hiding how much I want this.

He says, "Bailey, I want us to be real. It's been two years and that's long enough. I want everything tonight."

10

———

We must have forgotten to pull the blinds because the sun is super bright as it pours through the window the next morning. Damn deserts. Don't they know I need my beauty rest? Especially after last night?

∼

No, I'm screwing around. Let's back up.

∼

"I WANT EVERYTHING."

Gordo is bossy. Not with his words. After that final declaration, he says very little. But his hands, his mouth, even the way he breathes all make it pretty clear what he's looking for, and I am only too happy to give it to him.

I wish I could say he rips his clothes off, buttons flying, but that would be a tragedy for a well-cut piece of cotton. Instead, he sits up on his heels and undoes each button, until the open shirt frames his fuzzy chest and broad, flat belly. He unrolls the sleeves, smoothing them down.

"Goodbye, buddies," I say to his forearms. "I'll see you soon."

Gordo arches an eyebrow and laughs softly before pulling his shirt off and laying it gently on the coffee table. My legs are still trapped underneath him, but I push up onto my elbows, and he gives me ample room to sit up all the way. He's so tall that my mouth basically comes up to the centre of his torso, and that's good enough for me, as I plant kisses into his chest hair before moving to find his nipples.

He hisses when I drag my tongue over the first one. I glance up, and he's watching me, silent like an oak. He grunts when I bite down gently, tugging with my teeth, but when I check again, his mouth has fallen open and he's panting.

Good enough. I spend some time introducing myself to his other nipple while my hands get to know the rest of him. The muscled domes of his shoulders, the thick cords along his spine. He buries his fingers in my hair and lifts me up to kiss him, and I wonder why we've waited so long to do this.

He waits patiently when I start to undo his belt. My palms are unexpectedly shaky as I slip the leather through the loop. His pants fit him perfectly, and the outline of his erection is very clear in the material. When I pull down the zipper and push his pants over his hips, the very tip of him peeks out over the top of the elastic waistband of his boxer briefs.

"Jesus Christ, Gordo," I say. He runs a hand across his groin, grasping himself. In his palm, his dick looks manageable. When I brush my hand over the back of his and he lets me take over, the size of this . . . um . . . undertaking becomes clearer.

But Gordo rumbles, sort of like the way I think a lion might purr as I work him gently, letting the material slide over him as he gets—oh fuck—even bigger, and the happy sound makes me want to please him. I can do this. I can do it for him.

Except then a thought occurs to me. "Shit, we don't have any lube." When I packed, it wasn't the sort of thing I expected to need on this trip.

If only *past me* could see us now.

Gordo says, "I have lube. And condoms."

I stare up at him with all the wonder of a child on Christmas morning. "You do?"

He reaches down to the pants that are hanging by his knees and fiddles until he finds the pocket. He pulls out a couple small packs of lube and some condoms.

Amazing. "You planned ahead?" Something about the idea that Gordo has been planning to seduce me since before we left makes this all that much more exciting.

"Called down to the front desk while you were in the shower."

Well, that works too.

"You pressed zero and said 'I need lube and condoms so I can fuck my roommate, even though he's been completely oblivious to my sexuality and intentions for the last two years. Don't mind me, I want him anyway'?"

Gordo shakes his head. "Not in so many words."

No, I wouldn't think so. Gordo would never be so frank.

But the details are important right now. I'm feeling greedy. "You're going to fuck me, though, right? I mean, I'll top if you want, but I really—"

He stops that question with a kiss that makes my head spin before he pushes me back down onto the sofa.

"Oh, I'm going to fuck you. Been wanting to for the longest time."

My dick has slipped under a fold of the robe again, but it is doing its darndest to find the light. I bite my lip when Gordo pulls the tie loose. He spreads it open so my body is exposed. My erection pops up with a cheery hello, bobbing in greeting, and I clench just to make it do it again, and watch as Gordo's face breaks out in a satisfied smile.

"Like what you see?" I ask.

"You're so pretty, Bailey," Gordo says. "Knew you would be."

We're going to have to get a sofa like this at home. I can tell already. Gordo stretches out on his belly, kissing down my stomach and along my thighs. His beard tickles and it makes me jump and laugh, but his hands hold me down with an easy strength that has me shaking. He bites little kisses along the insides of my thighs, and I nearly poke him in the eye as I try to get my dick in his mouth, but he doesn't seem to mind. He takes me in one of his big hands and draws my tip along the flat of his pink tongue, and oh my God, as long as I live, I will never forget the image of Gordo, head between my legs, eyes on mine, as he slides me into the wet heat of his mouth.

"Oh. Gordo. God." He might be divine. His mouth sure as hell is. He slides up and down, tongue doing magical things that make my brain go to putty. So much better than top-secret jerk offs in the bathroom. My whole body rolls as he slides down to take me all the way to the back of his throat. He gags and releases me, giving me an apologetic smile, and I don't know what he has to be sorry for, especially not when he swirls the tip of his tongue under the crown of my dick, sending lightning into my groin and all over my body.

"Please. Please, yeah. Please," I beg. His breath wafts over my slick shaft as he licks down the underside before getting acquainted with my balls and taint. I know where he's headed, and I can't wait. I shrug free of the robe's sleeves so I can help him, pulling my legs back to give him access.

The first time someone rimmed me, I nearly had an out-of-body experience. I definitely came before he ever got a finger or a cock in my ass. Something about it, the heat, the spit, the gentle exploration as Gordo pushes the tip of his tongue inside me . . . It's always been my favourite. I don't hold back my praise as he slowly works me open. I hope the walls in this hotel are plenty soundproof.

"Gordo. Yes. Oh God, Gordo."

God and Gordo are both very, very good. I've basically got my knees pulled up around my ears. Gordo has his hands under my lower back, holding me up so he can eat my ass exactly the way he wants.

But with that comes certain risks. My balls are getting tight, and my cock drips pre-come on my belly like a leaky garden hose.

I say, "Gordo. Gordo, I'm going to come."

I whine when he lets me go. My hole flexes, looking for stimulation, and I shiver as his spit dries on my skin.

He says, "Not yet," and the words are a rumble that means I nearly come anyway. But then a pack of lube lands on my belly and I look up to see Gordo resuming his place in the corner of the sectional. Somewhere along the way, he's taken his pants and underwear off, so he's a mat of red hair and a proud, thick cock that makes my stomach clench. He's got a condom between two fingers and another sachet of lube.

He says, "Open yourself up. I wanna see."

I mean, I'm pretty relaxed already. Gordo was very thorough. But as he strokes himself in one of his massive hands, I reason that a little more prep never hurt anybody and tear open the lube.

I'll admit, I've never found this part particularly sexy. Tongues, yes. Fingers? Meh. I can take it or leave it. But I do my best for Gordo, and he definitely seems to enjoy it, watching intently as I slide in two, then three fingers, rocking down onto my hand, showing how much I want him and how ready I am.

He must agree because he rolls the condom down his length,

then slicks his dick up more. He's so big, and I have every right to be afraid.

I can't take my eyes off his erection, and he says, "We'll go slow. You can be on top." And oh Jesus, I hadn't even thought about the other option. Maybe I'm too much of a control freak, but I sort of figured I'd get to ride him. Lying on my back while he pushes into me might be too much.

He lets his thighs fall open, arms over the back of the sofa. He crooks one finger toward me, and my chest goes all fluttery with anticipation. I crawl into his lap, straddling him and kissing him, letting him know I'm here and I'm ready. I reach back and position myself so the head of his cock is at my ass. Jesus, I don't know if I can do this.

He kisses me again, lips soft and warm. I let my fingers run through his hair, which is stiff with whatever product he used. All for me. He's done all of this. The hair, the clothes, every-thing. For me.

When he pushes past the ring of muscle, I cry out, and his hands come to my sides, holding me still.

"Sorry." He really does sound like he's apologizing, and we can't have that, so instead we have some more kissing, and slowly I work him inside me. The stretch is amazing. I feel drunk, even though by now most of the buzz from the drinks at the club have worn off.

"Gordo."

"I'm here," he says, and finally I settle all the way down into the cradle of his thighs and his groan is the most perfect sound of satisfaction.

We go slow. Little movements as I rock my hips. Someday, I want to do this like I imagined last night, with me bent over and him pounding into me, telling me filthy things. But tonight, I want to get to know him, this new Gordo who has been waiting here all along.

Finally, he takes control. We reposition so I have my back to him. He's like a big fuzzy cradle that holds me in place while he spreads my legs open with his thighs and pumps into me.

"Oh. Jesus. Oh my God." I'm not much for religion, but I'd go to church for this. He's moving in and out of me with long strokes, and I'm helpless to do anything but take him, and it's so, so perfect. When he takes hold of my cock and starts to jerk me in time with his thrusts, the stimulation is too much, the hot, wet friction overwhelming on top of the shock when he bumps against my prostate.

"It's okay," I say, stilling his grip. "I'm good without that."

He lets go, and instead he latches on to my shoulder with his mouth, and I am going to have a Gordo-sized hickey there in the morning, but at least I can cover it with a shirt. I press a hand to the side of his head, tilting mine back so he can have all the room he wants as I work myself up and down as fast as I can.

"Gordo. Gordo. GordoGordoGordo. I—" But I don't have time to tell him before I'm coming, back bowing against him as my cock jerks and spurts all over my belly. He's moving faster now too. Still not rough, but with purpose. His hands grip my hips as he pumps into me. He's growling against my skin, and I can't stop the tumble of words that come out, praising him, encouraging him. His orgasm is a grunt as he drops his forehead to my neck. He trembles and shakes underneath me, and we should talk about sexual health and if we truly need condoms, because I want to feel the wet heat of him as he unloads inside me.

I need help disengaging. My legs are like noodles. In fact, my whole body is limp as he lifts me off him. He kisses me, laughing softly into my cheek, and all I can do is pet his chest hair and tell him he's a good boy. Or maybe I say I'm a good boy. I don't know. Everything is hazy and heavy, except for me, apparently, because he carries me up to the giant bed. We're both naked, and it's so funny that twenty-four hours ago I was triple checking he was okay to sleep in the same bed as me, and now I can't imagine being anywhere else.

My head fits right under his chin and he spoons around me. My ass throbs and it's the best feeling in the world.

"See you in the morning?" I say.

He tucks his knees behind mine and drapes a giant arm over my hip.

"You bet."

11

———

We must have forgotten to pull the blinds because the sun is super bright as it pours through the window in the morning. Damn deserts. Don't they know I need my beauty rest? Especially after last night?

May I continue now?

I wake up and I am sweating. Like I'm soaked. Also, I can't breathe. Part of it is the dry air in Vegas. Part of it is that my face is smooshed into Gordo's chest, and I'm sure many people have been smothered to death by pillows less fluffy than this.

But also, it's kinda nice. More than nice. I snuggle in, finding new places for our skin to stick together. Gordo's big arms tighten around my back, and I want to stay here forever. Maybe, along with a sectional and the fancy showerhead, we can get one of these giant king beds at home too. If we're sharing a room, we need to make some space.

I'm surprisingly unbothered by the idea of Gordo moving in with me. I mean, he moved in years ago. What's a change of bedroom? More places for the monitor lizards to chill.

"What time is it?" Gordo asks.

I roll, fumbling for my phone on the side table. It's a long reach, but I don't want to leave the haven of Gordo's embrace.

Except . . . "Goddammit." Nearly eight. First meeting of the day starts in half an hour.

Gordo kisses the back of my neck. "Time to go?"

I need a shower at least.

"Can I ask you something?" I say, buying a few more minutes that I'll probably pay for later.

"Anything."

"You said last night that you used to be like me. That you worked too much to have a relationship. What did you mean?"

His eyes go serious. He smooths a hair down on my forehead. Gordo says, "That's a long story. Let's not talk about it now."

"There's no group dinner tonight," I say. "We can talk about it then."

Getting out of bed and taking a shower is the worst. I don't want to start my day. Things get a little better when, a minute after I've turned on the water, the shower door slides open and Gordo steps in behind me.

"What are you going to do today?" I ask.

"Elias and I are going to the aquarium."

I snort. "You two seem pretty friendly."

"He's nice. He likes animals."

"He can't be that nice if he's dating Jake the—" My comment gets cut off as Gordo massages shampoo into my hair. I have to let his body take my weight because the sensation is heavenly. He turns me and tips my head back to rinse, and our two naked and very erect cocks bump against each other. Gordo leans in to kiss me, but I hiss when one of his powerful hands finds my ass.

"Sore?" he asks.

"A little." I don't want to turn down what he's offering, but he really was very big, and it's been a while since I've been with anyone.

"My fault," he says.

"No. It's fine. I'll just—" But he clearly doesn't hear whatever I'm about to offer. Instead, Gordo drops to his knees on the tile and takes care of my aching cock with his mouth.

Surprising no one, I'm late to the first session of the morning. Actually, the surprise is probably that I'm only five minutes late. The way Gordo left me a twitching blissed-out mess in the bottom of the shower, I could have been much, much later.

I slide into an empty chair at one of the folding tables near the back of the room, balancing my laptop and a paper cup of very expensive and very good cappuccino. A few heads turn toward me, but no one gives me a hard time as I settle in. I ache unexpectedly but not unpleasantly when my ass hits the solid plastic, but the sensation lets me relive the highlight reel from the night before.

Being with Gordo makes sense. Maybe we've been together all this time and I never realized. Not sexually, but sex isn't the only thing that makes a couple. It's not like either one of us has any friends to speak of. I hang out with customers and guys from work. Gordo does whatever it is Gordo does, but somehow I don't think it's hanging out with a secret social circle he's never bothered to tell me about. The bottom line is, we aren't only roommates and never have been. We give each other space to be our own people, but at the end of the night, when everything else sucks, the thing I want most is Gordo, one of his cupcakes, stories about whichever corn snake he rescued that day, and now—finally—his hungry hands on my body.

So of course, as I'm stitching together the pieces of this new reality, who slides into the seat next to me, but Jake the Jerk?

"Hey, friend," he says with a leer. "How was your night?"

Fuck him. I'm so over Jake and his questions.

"Better once I got the barf off my shoes," I say, then make a point of turning on my laptop and taking meticulous notes as the man at the front—some Senior Regional VP from Colorado—talks about redistributing sales territories and strategic industry targets. For all they swore the buyout wasn't going to change our jobs, less and less about our day-to-day operations looks like the job I have given myself to for the last nine years.

Jake makes a sympathetic noise. "Yeah, that was embarrassing. Looks bad for the company, you know?"

Considering Jake was almost as drunk as Lachlan was, he doesn't have much of a leg to stand on here. I give him a tight smile that hopefully he takes as agreement and definitely is meant as encouragement that he should shut the hell up.

He doesn't. Instead, he leans close to me—closer than anyone but Gordo should—and says, "So listen. I talked to Ed."

"Good for you." I keep typing. According to the guy at the front, Canada is now going to be one big territory, and Jake may have Ed's ear, but Ed's inbox is going to have a very long letter from in me in it as soon as I get home about why that plan is a terrible one.

"He agrees that your office is struggling."

I stiffen. Here comes the hammer. I hate the idea of letting Jake win anything, but if he tells me I'm not cutting it, I'll be happy to walk out of here right now. Maybe catch Gordo before he and Elias head out to the aquarium. Elias will have to take a rain check, because Gordo and I are spending the rest of the day in bed.

"Because the numbers are unreasonable. You can't just set new sales targets and walk away," I say under my breath, because if I'm out, the least I can do is try to make things easier for the people left behind.

"Oh, I agree," Jake says. "An integration like this is all about strong leadership."

Which Jake will never be. He's too slippery. Too self-interested.

He says, "Lachlan's out."

My fingers skitter on the keyboard. "What?"

"I spoke to Ed," Jake says, voice smooth like snakeskin. "He agrees that Lachlan isn't the man for the job."

My pulse is racing. Lachlan has been my boss for six years. We came up together. He's been a friend and a mentor, and yes, he's in over his head right now, but we all are.

"What are you talking about?" I say.

Jake smiles. He has my attention and he knows he's won. He says, "Monday morning. As soon as everyone's back at the office, we'll pull the plug."

I can't believe what I'm hearing. "Is this about last night? That's not fair. Everyone has a story about overdoing it on a trip like this."

Jake shakes his head. "It's been on the radar for a few weeks. We wanted to see how the dust settled, but it's not working."

My stomach tightens. The cappuccino tastes like mud when I take a sip. I glance around for Lachlan, but I don't see him. Hopefully he's still in his room, sleeping off his hangover instead of sitting in here like a chump, trying to figure out how he's going to save our office when he's already been fed to the lions.

Jake says, "We want you to take his place."

Motherfucker.

I don't say anything. What I really want to do is leap to my feet, run the hell out of here, strip out of my clothes in front of the Bellagio and go for a swim in the fountain.

Instead, I open up the old school solitaire game on my laptop—seriously, how is this still installed on every computer? —and play a few hands. I suck at solitaire, but it gives me something to do while my mind races.

Finally, Jake says, "Did you hear me?" and the question is at least some small comfort, because I made him repeat himself, and Jake doesn't like to be forced to do anything.

I nod.

He says, "And?"

I say, "I'll have to think about it."

Jake snorts. "Sure you do." He jerks his head toward the guy with the PowerPoint presentation up front. "As of Monday, it's all one territory, and I'm offering it to you. You'd manage sales for all of Canada."

I glare at him. Let him know how I truly feel. "And work for you."

He smirks. "We're adults. We'll let bygones be bygones. We need to do a quarterly conference call to check in, and otherwise you never have to see me."

It can't be that easy. "That's it?"

Jake folds his hands in front of him like the matter is already settled. "Ed's committed to making this merger work. I said you were the best man for the job."

Yeah, right. Jake's never said anything so kind about me in his entire life.

But when I glance at him again, his smile is still cool, but there's no hint of teasing in his face. His eyes are totally serious.

"Me?" I say. "All of Canada?"

"All of it. You send me reports that show things are getting better, and I'll stay out of your hair. Don't care how you do it."

I shudder, thinking about the analyses and targets that have been coming across my desk for the last few weeks. It feels like a mountain.

But haven't I been training for this my whole career? I would never squeeze Lachlan out. I sort of thought we'd find a way to work together. But I have a team too. People who report to me and depend on BGS&M to put food on their table every month. More people now, if I accept what Jake is offering.

"I want to talk to Ed," I say. "Look him in the eye and make sure he's on board with this."

Jake nods. "Absolutely. I'll set it up. We'll have a drink tomorrow afternoon."

Somehow, I don't feel better. I sort of thought he'd try to put me off. That he wanted to slip something by me. But if he actually can get me in front of Ed to talk about it, it must be official.

He holds out his hand, and I expect the skin to be scaly and cold when I shake it, but it's warm and alive, and somehow that's worse.

"We're going to be great together," Jake says.

I'm worried he's right.

I could get used to coming home to Gordo.

The meetings go late, and I have to beg off the round of drinks after. I haven't seen Gordo in close to ten hours, and I am nearly crawling out of my skin.

Fortunately, the feeling is mutual. As I let myself in, Gordo is on me in seconds.

"Hi," I say, but then I'm in the air and Gordo's carrying me through the room. "Miss me?"

He doesn't answer. Just kisses me silly and sets me down by the window.

"Clothes off," he says, but I glance over my shoulder, then smile at him.

"I have a better idea." I drop to my knees and slowly pull off the still-damp and still-tiny swim trunks he's wearing. "Put your hands on the glass."

Turns out, as much as Gordo likes watching the fountain, watching it while he's not allowed to look at his boyfriend while he gets a blow job is even more fun. For both of us.

Am I his boyfriend? Is that what we are? This feels serious.

Way more than friends with benefits. Boyfriends with benefits, which is to say we have the benefit of already being friends.

"How was your day?" he asks as he slides his trunks back on.

My post-blow glow fizzles a bit at the thought of my conversation with Jake. I wave Gordo off. "Boring. Meetings. You know. How was yours? The aquarium was fun?"

And Gordo launches into a discussion of the relative merits of the aquarium versus other ones he's been to, and whether or not marine animals should be kept in captivity like that at all, or if research should be limited to what can be done in the field.

I love how much Gordo loves learning. How passionate he gets about the weirdest things. Like, *"Did you know there are some species of fish that live in caves at the bottom of the ocean where light never ever gets, and so these fish have evolved to have no eyes?"*

No, Gordo, I did not know that, and the idea of eyeless fish is simultaneously fascinating, terrifying, and a little gross.

Fortunately, the Gordo marine biology lecture takes us all the way to dinner. Technically, although the retreat has no formal meal scheduled tonight, we were encouraged to make plans with coworkers and people we'd met from other offices. But I'm overwhelmed by Jake's proposal and Lachlan never showed up today, so I'm choosing to forgo the teambuilding in favour of building up this little team of two that Gordo and I are forging.

We find a Chinese place that's made to look like a vintage Shanghai nightclub. Old Chinese movies play on TVs overhead. I've noticed Gordo doesn't drink much, so we order tea made from flowers that bloom in pots of hot water and plates full of dumplings and sautéed greens. Gordo wields his chopsticks with deft fingers, even though they look like toothpicks in his strong hands. He gets soup in his beard and wipes it off with his thumb, which he licks, and I have to bunch my napkin up in my lap and take a gulp of tea so hot it nearly scalds the back of my throat before I'm able to form coherent sentences again.

I say, "Where'd you learn to use those?"

He holds up the chopsticks. "These?" For once, Gordo's seemingly permanent cheer cracks a bit. He sets them down and wipes his hands. "I guess we should talk about that."

"Talk about what?"

"You know Rolls-Royce hasn't made rocket engines in five or six years, right?"

"Of course not. Why would I know that? I was trying to impress Jake and remembered that YouTube thing you made me watch. But what does that have to do with anything?"

Gordo lets out a long, gusty sigh that sends ripples over the top of his teacup. He says, "Because I did an internship at Rolls-Royce in the aerospace division when I was in university."

I choke on a dumpling. "Excuse me?"

He shrugs as though it's no big deal, but it definitely is. I can't imagine Gordo using words like "intern" and "aerospace," much less being a part of them. I sort of imagine Gordo did a semester somewhere, realized it wasn't for him, spent years backpacking across the world, learning from wise men and poets, before he finally decided his calling was saving defenceless reptiles and making sure someone scrubs down our shower at least once a month.

"I have advanced degrees in electrical and aeronautical engineering."

"You do?"

It's like we've switched roles. Normally, I'm the one with all the information and Gordo trailing after, repeating what I've said because the words only make sense in my head, not the real world.

"I worked at Rolls-Royce and then at Boeing. Seattle has

great Chinese food." He wiggles the chopsticks in my direction. "Then I got a job at Microsoft and—"

"Wait, wait." I put a hand on his wrist. "*The* Microsoft. Like you know Bill Gates?"

He shakes his head. "Not really. We only met a few times."

"A few times?" I should have ordered a drink after all.

"And then I went out on my own and worked in development."

Now he's lost me. "What kind of development?"

"Programming, mostly. My business partners handled most of the customer-facing stuff. They let me stay behind a computer and I managed the technical side." He runs a hand over his throat, like his collar is too tight. "We designed a chip that was supposed to be used for commercial airline navigation, but then one day we got approached by a defence contractor. They offered us a lot of money to buy the patent and IP."

"How much money?" Suddenly I'm remembering him the night before, chatting up my coworkers and shaking Ed Morton's hand like he had met men like him before, and now I'm wondering if he has. I mean, *Bill Gates*. But who else?

Gordo says, "I didn't want to sell. Didn't want what I'd built going to something that might hurt people. So the guys bought me out and sold the chip."

Oh. I don't like the sound of that. "They forced you out?" I'm thinking about poor Lachlan, who's a dead man walking and doesn't even know it.

"They paid me for my time and equity. And I had a good lawyer, so I still got a cut when they sold the patent. But I didn't want the money. That's how I started the reptile rescue."

My brain is spinning, doing math, realigning what I know, struggling to envision Gordo behind a lab bench or at a computer, building something that flies jets—actually, I can almost see that—and sitting at a table with black-suited lawyers demanding his cut of the cash—that part is harder.

"How much could it possibly cost to run a rescue?" I laugh, trying to sound casual.

"The animals I bring home to our place don't cost much. They're the healthiest. But not everyone we take in is doing as well, and eventually it became easier to open our own clinic rather than paying vet bills every time someone brought us a sick tortoise."

I blink. "You own a clinic? Like with veterinarians?"

"A few now. It started out that what we made off pet owners covered the cost of the rescue, but then it turned out to be a pretty good business model. Everyone has a pet that needs looking after, and our rates are fair. So now we've got animal hospitals and rescue volunteers in five cities in Canada and another sixteen in the States."

"And you, what?" I'm still not sure I'm understanding. "You take a percentage off the top and live on that?"

Gordo laughs. "No. They're not that profitable."

"Oh. Okay."

"I live off the interest of what I got paid in the buyout."

I was about to bite into a wonton, but it slips through my chopsticks and lands back in my soup with a splat.

I'm not afraid to talk about money. We make a lot of it at BGS&M. And while it's rude to compare paycheques over dinner, if I'm going to be with Gordo, I think I need a little more context.

"Gordo," I say, trying to keep my voice calm and quiet. The restaurant isn't exactly busy, but I'm not about to ask him to show me his bank balance in a public place. "When we're talking about the buyout, how big are we talking?"

He presses his lips together. "Pretty big."

"Like . . . how many zeroes, would you say, before you get to a real number?" God. Maybe I am being rude. I don't care what the number is. I have a good job. But I'm learning things about Gordo here pretty quickly, and I think the answer to this question is going to tell me a lot about how and why he lives the way he does.

He squirms a bit in his seat, and I almost tell him not to worry about it, but before I can, he says, "Seven. No, eight. Depends on interest and how much I have to spend flying animals around the country in any given year."

I have to run the sequence in my head a few times before I picture a number clearly in my head. Eight is . . .

"Holy shit. That's a lot of zeroes."

"It is. I worked hard for them. But I don't want something I do to be used for things I don't believe in again. I didn't like playing those games. All the strategizing and backbiting. So now I do what I actually like."

Yes, he does. He shuffles around our condo and microwaves mice. He disappears for days at a time to . . . what? Check in on his clinics and the volunteers who support the same things he does, probably.

I chew on my wonton as I consider what to say next that won't be weird. Finally, I say, "So you're what people call independently wealthy?"

"I guess so." The corner of his mouth twitches. "Can we talk about something else?"

"Yes." I let out a relieved breath. "Yes, we absolutely can."

We talk about food. Gordo likes the mushroom dumplings best. I like the pork. We talk about animals. Gordo still wants to see the mustangs, and I don't know how we're going to do that, but I promise we'll make it happen. We talk about going to see a show after dinner, but Gordo finds my calf with the side of his foot under the table and makes it clear that we've been out in public for long enough.

I can definitely get used to coming home with Gordo. We fall into the bed and into each other—Gordo more into me more than the other way around—and again I regret that it took us so long to get here. Because Gordo's body on mine, as he pushes into me and runs tickly wet kisses along my back, is pretty much the best thing over. We have a chat about condoms and health status, and when he comes this time, there's no latex, and the smear of his spunk on my thighs as he pulls out is pretty much perfect, as is the careful way he cleans me up when we take our second shower of the day together.

We fall asleep, me tucked against him in a way that is already becoming familiar, and I'm sorry that we don't have many more days left in Vegas. Because we don't need to leave the things we've said to each other behind. They don't have to stay here. But the real world won't quite be the same. Gordo says he doesn't want to live this life. The corporate one with the games and the strategies. But I've got a job offer on the table that will push me into it deeper than ever before. As he snores softly in my ear, I wonder if the life I lead will be enough for him. It's the life I've been working for, but it's one Gordo walked away from.

I'm not sure how I get to have both.

13

W aking up to sex with Gordo is pretty much fantastic. Only slightly less fantastic—but still utterly amazing—is waking up to Gordo letting himself back into the room with a tray of coffee cups and a bag full of pastries that are ninety percent butter and still warm.

"Is this heaven?" I say as I pull apart a flaky chocolate croissant.

"It's Vegas," Gordo says as he kisses my bare shoulder.

"Would you come here again?"

He's lying on his side, propped up on one elbow, and the morning light on his skin as he glances out the window is pretty much art. He says, "If you wanted to."

Sounds like a no to me. I can live with that. Vegas is fun, but I think Gordo and I could find new places to explore together.

But first, I have a final workshop, a farewell lunch, and a meeting with Jake the Jerk and Ed Morton. I groan and flop back down on the bed. Gordo takes that as an invitation to crawl on top of me. I love the gentle way he holds me, even as our bodies demand filthy things.

But I have to go to work.

I leave Gordo tangled up in the sheets, all naked temptation. I'm not usually one to get all swoony, but maybe I can take a few extra days off work so I can spend them all with Gordo, instead of constantly being pulled away.

Lachlan is sitting on a bench outside the conference room. His shirt is wrinkled and his hair looks like it hasn't seen a comb in weeks.

"Hey," I say with a laugh. "Are you and your liver on speaking terms again?"

He stares up at me with vacant eyes. He smells about as good as he looks.

"You okay?" I ask.

He blinks, and his internal lights turn back on. He launches to his feet and grabs me by the sleeve, dragging me the way I've come.

"What's going on?" I have to half run to keep up with him.

"We can't talk about it here."

We go out to the pool deck, still mostly empty. It's cool before the desert sun has a chance to warm things up again. Lachlan sits me down on one of the loungers. We must look weird in our business casual. An attendant in a windbreaker comes over to ask if we need anything, but Lachlan waves him off.

"What happened?" I say. "Where have you been?"

Lachlan shakes his head. "There's a coup."

"A what?"

"The other company." He runs his hands through his hair, and it's obvious where the mad scientist look came from. "They're taking over."

I snort. "Think they already did that, buddy. Did you miss the memo?"

"No." He braces on his elbows, breathing hard. "They're changing everything."

I still don't get what he's trying to tell me. Nothing he's said is news. From the targets to the territories, nothing is the way it was before.

"We'll get used to it," I say.

Lachlan shivers. He's only wearing a collared shirt, no jacket, and now that I think about it, it might be the same one he was wearing two days ago at the dinner. Has he been wandering the Strip this whole time? Debauching himself and losing money at craps?

He says, "They promised. They called me before the meeting. They said there was nothing to worry about." He leans back, arching away from me like he's struggling to breathe. "We can't keep going this way."

Oh, man. I can't tell him. He's in rough shape, and I shudder to think what he'll do if I say he's already lost his job. He's been the closest thing I've had to a friend for a long time—except for Gordo, obviously—and I hate to see him like this. If he knows the job he's devoted so much to is gone, he might go piss away everything he has at the blackjack table or go step out into traffic, or stand out in front of the hotel and wait for the death ray to get him.

I say, "Lachlan, it's going to be okay. Why don't you take another day off? Get some rest. I'll tell them you're sick."

"Jake." He's rambling now. "He's a snake. Jake the snake. You can't trust him."

"I know," I say, trying to help him to his feet. He's really shaking now, and I don't think it's only from the breeze.

"We have to work together. Keep him out. He can't run things."

"I know." My only hope is that what he said was the truth. Quarterly meetings and otherwise I can do things my way. I'm sorry Lachlan won't be there, but maybe this is the best thing for him. He's clearly under even more stress than I realized. He should talk to Gordo, get some tips about engaging in a whole-life makeover. Of course, unless Lachlan's sitting on a trust fund I don't know about, he may not be able to finance a pet-rescue plan, but surely he'll find a job that isn't going to put him in an early grave or decades of therapy.

I walk him all the way up to his floor. He talks the entire time. Weird run-on sentences about how people are supposed to keep their promises and how he should have been a dentist. It sucks that he's so unhappy.

He's already stripping out of his clothes as the door to his room swings shut, and I hope he starfishes into his bed and stays there for hours. I'll have to make sure he gets on his flight okay tomorrow.

I stare at his closed door for a long time. No part of me wants to go back to work. The idea of being in a room with Jake for one more minute makes my skin itch, but it will look so bad if both Lachlan and I are MIA.

Movement in the corner of my eye catches my attention. I turn, and standing at the end of the hall is a dog.

No, seriously. A real live chihuahua, with big ears, pointy little nose, and four paws braced on the floor like I've caught him trying to break into someone's room.

The floor is weirdly quiet. Just the hum of the air conditioner. I glance over my shoulder, but I'm alone. Only me and the little dog who, when I take one step forward, springs into action and takes off.

"Hey." I hurry after it. The dog is fast. Those little legs can go when it wants to.

I didn't exactly plan to spend time today chasing after runaway chihuahuas, but what else am I supposed to do? The dog weighs about four pounds and this hotel has sixty stories. Clearly no one is looking for it, and that's weird.

"Hey. Hey, come here." I bend to catch it, but it scampers

away, always checking over its shoulder to make sure I'm still there. Yeah. This game is hilarious.

Finally, we reach the end of the hall and the thing has nowhere else to go. I half expect to be bitten for my trouble, but when I pick up the dog, it snuggles into my chest, panting happily.

Well, shit. Now what do I do? I stand in the silent hall, waiting for someone to burst out of their room as they realize their dog is gone. But nothing happens. I can't very well go door to door, knocking to see if someone's home and if they're missing a chihuahua. It's Vegas. Who knows what lurks behind any of these walls?

I'll take it down to the front desk. Seems like the reasonable plan.

"They'll know what to do," I say to the dog, who gazes up at me with shiny eyes. It stretches up to lick my chin, and I can't help but think about Gordo and his snakes and wonder if any of them have ever licked him in thanks for all the hard work he's put into making their lives better.

The dog sucks in a deep inhale that seems to double its body size, before letting out a long-contented sigh.

"Yeah," I say with a smile. "Chill. We're going to figure this out."

I manage to get the button for the elevator pushed without jostling my cargo too much. No doubt the people at the front desk know which guests have brought pets with them and who this dog belongs to.

The bell dings and the elevator door slides open. A man is getting off, so I step back to give him some room.

"Where the hell have you been!"

I glance up, and he's staring at me with shocked eyes.

"What—" But before I can even ask, he lunges for me. I dodge back, but the hall is narrow and there isn't much place to go. I don't have time to work up a protest, and then he rips the dog out of my arms.

"You scared me!" he says. He's a big man. Not as big as Gordo, but solid. And now he's shaking with relief as the dog wriggles in his arms and makes desperate, happy whimpering noises as it tries to kiss his entire face with its tiny tongue.

"Don't ever do that again." He doesn't even look at me as he gets back on the elevator. The dog seems to whine in agreement, and then the door slides shut again, leaving me alone.

I don't—

I don't know what to say.

Did that just happen?

The drying doggy spit on my chin says yes, but—

I kinda wish Gordo had been here so he could corroborate my story for future retellings.

A desperate giggle tries to escape, and I clap my hand over my mouth to keep it down. I should have brought the dog to Lachlan. Then I'd have a witness, and Lachlan would have something to snuggle with and maybe cheer him up.

But the man in the elevator seemed so relieved. How did that even happen? The dog made a break for it on another floor and has been having wild adventures up and down this hotel. The way the man clutched at it said he might never let that little doggy's feet touch the floor ever again.

The giggle, trapped in my throat, makes tears leak out of the corners of my eyes.

Shit, am I crying now? Over a dog?

But yup. Here I am, when I'm supposed to be in another workshop about executive leadership or some bullshit, and instead I'm standing in front of the elevator fucking crying.

I need to get my head on straight. They'll be eyeing me like Lachlan soon. The diseased gazelle at the back of the pack.

I pull myself together. Text Gordo. *You'll never guess what happened.* But he doesn't reply, so I guess he's gone out. Looking for a property to buy so he can set up a Vegas branch of his clinics? Maybe he already has a Vegas branch. God. There's so much I don't know about him, and I feel like he knows everything there is about me.

No one seems to notice or care when I sneak into the workshop. Jake's giving the talk today. His gaze slides over me as I enter, and he smiles to himself, but he keeps talking. I sit down in the back of the room, slumping as low as I can in my chair. Fuck taking notes. Fuck planning next steps. I'm not changing anymore for these assholes. They clearly know the value I offer to the organization. Jake's getting his quarterly calls and I'm getting on with my life. I run Canada now. All of it.

When the talk is over, I basically leap out of my seat and head for the door. Gordo still hasn't answered my text, but I'm pretty sure if I go lie in bed and send him a few tasteful nudes—okay, maybe not so tasteful. Gordo's the man of mystery in this relationship, not me—he'll be back soon enough.

Except Jake must have discovered teleportation, because before I can leave, he's already standing by the door.

"Well, hey there," he says.

"Hi. Great talk." I go to push past him, but he sticks to me like Velcro.

"Going somewhere?"

"I left something in my room," I say, trying to pick up the pace, but we're trapped walking behind two slowpokes from some regional branch office who don't know I'm about to mow them down.

"Good," Jake says, without missing a step. "For a second, I thought you forgot about our lunch with Ed."

"We're having drinks later," I say.

"Mm, no. I tried drinks, but he's busy. Didn't you get my email?"

Goddammit. I glance down at my phone, and sure enough, there's a calendar invite from Jake. *Lunch with Ed.* After Lachlan and the dog and everything else, I didn't even bother checking my email this morning.

"Fine." I stop so fast that Jake trips on the rug, and that at least makes me happy.

"Fine?" He looks surprised.

"Yeah, let's go."

His smile is cunning. I hate him so much. "What about the thing in your room?"

I picture Gordo, whose smile is always kind and who brought me breakfast in bed because that's who he is. Bringing him here was the best and worst idea. Best, because obviously. Worst, because I can't stay focused on work for more than a second without missing him. If I'd known how my "please pretend to be my boyfriend" plan was going to end up, I'd have never suggested it. He could have pined peacefully from the comfort of home, and we would have figured our shit out eventually.

"It can wait," I say. "Lead the way. Let's have lunch with Ed."

14

Jake takes me to a sports bar. It's so dark I can barely see. The only light comes from the floor-to-ceiling wall of TV screens that show every sporting event currently happening around the globe, from football to stock car racing to bowling. The flickering lights make me squint. Ed's got a beer and a burger the size of his head as we sit down.

"Jack! Good to see you."

I notice Jake doesn't correct him as we take our seats.

"Ed, this is Bailey Baldwin from the Toronto office. We talked about him."

"Yes, yes." Ed wipes his hands on a paper napkin before reaching over to shake. "Heard great things about you. Glad you're willing to hear what Jack here had to say."

"Yes. Thanks, sir."

"Can I get you a drink?" A server stops by the table.

"Tomato juice," I say.

"Better be vodka in that tomato juice," Ed says with a grin.

I glance at Jake, who casually orders a double rum and coke.

Sure, why not? "Manhattan," I say. "Extra cherries."

God, except I'm thinking of Gordo playfully stealing cherries off a plastic sword on an airplane. At the time it was annoying. Now it seems erotic as hell.

"So." Ed claps his hands. "Canada. Jack says you're the man for the job."

Adrenaline pulses through me, but I do my best to sound confident when I say, "I think so, yes."

"Shame about the other one. What was his name? Lawrence?"

"Lachlan," I say.

"Yes, well, Jack said he wasn't the guy. He's been a big fan of yours from the beginning. Even before the deal was closed, he—"

"Bailey's been a company man since day one," Jake says. "Haven't you?"

Something prickles at the back of my mind. "I guess. I mean, Lachlan's been a friend. I wouldn't want him to—"

But Ed waves a hand as the server comes back with drinks. "Hard decisions have to be made. It's business, nothing personal. If you're going to run the whole Canadian territory, you've got to toughen up there." He punches my shoulder, and I do the bro chuckle that men do when they're uncomfortable and don't know what to say.

"Yeah, about that," I say. "You do realize that Canada is a pretty big place, right?"

More waving. "But not many people. Only so many companies for us to sell to. We've got to be smart about payroll here. Back in my day . . ."

Blah, blah, blah. I've heard these arguments all weekend. Talking about Canada like it's some backwater with a half dozen convenience stores. I work on my manhattan and nod whenever Ed glances at me. Jake stays remarkably silent, even though Ed insists on calling him Jack. Ed has almost definitely forgotten my name already, but I tell myself that none of it matters, because as soon as this meeting is over, I can go back to my room and have Gordo to fuck me senseless, and tomorrow we'll be on a plane back home and I don't have to see these two for at least a quarter and probably longer.

Ed goes on for so long, telling us stories of his glory days, big sales he's landed, golf games he's won, that our food arrives, and I have to order another drink to go with it.

"But you," Ed says, stabbing a finger in my direction, "we've been keeping an eye on you. Rising star. Everyone says so."

I should probably feel flattered. Instead, I feel creeped out, like Ed and possibly Jake have been watching me at the office through some creepy CCTV.

"I'll do my best," I say.

"I know you will." He seems satisfied. "But Canada is pretty big, as you said. So we've decided to set Jack up in the Toronto office."

What? The word is like a gunshot in my skull.

"What?" Jake sounds equally as shocked, which is gratifying at least.

"Yes." Ed grins. "We've been talking about it at head office. Jack is in charge of North American sales. No reason he couldn't be in Canada. And he's been such a big supporter of yours. Makes sense to keep you two close to each other. You'll make quite the team."

My stomach lurches. Jake. I glare at him, but he's gone pale, so I at least know this is as much of a surprise to him as it is to me. I can't take working in the same office as him. That wasn't the agreement. No amount of watching his discomfort now is going to make up for the agony of seeing his smug face every single day.

"Ed," Jake says, "I have far more people reporting to me in the U.S. than I do in Canada. Wouldn't it be more logical for me to stay—"

"Didn't you tell me you grew up in Canada?" Ed says.

Jake falters. "Well, yes, but—"

"Perfect! Then it will be like a homecoming. Barley, you'll make him welcome, right?"

Is he talking to me? This can't be happening. Out of everything, this is a disaster.

Somehow, my voice is steady long enough for me to say, "Sure."

And, as abruptly as it started, the meal ends. Ed stands up, clapping his hands. "Well, boys, this has been fun, but I have to catch a jet. Taking the wife to the coast. Jack, I'll call next week. Brandon, nice to meet you. Keep up the good work." Then he's gone, leaving Jake and me to gape in his wake.

Jake says, "I hate Canada."

I punch him.

No, I don't. I think about it. Like a lot. Instead, I down the rest of my drink and say, "Looks like lunch is on you. I'll see you at the office." Then I leave his smug face to pick up the bill.

My life is over. I cannot work with Jake every single day. The situation will be intolerable by Christmas. I'll fling myself out a window. No, I'll stab him with a pen, *then* I'll fling myself out a window. Fucking Jake the Jerk.

It's possible I lose a few hours at a slot machine. The spinning wheels, flashing lights, and the intermittent clanging when I win a fraction of the money I put into it are enough to park my brain, because the idea of what work will look like in very short order is painful.

Also, as an added bonus, drinks are free while you're in the casino. I order a couple more manhattans for good measure. They make everything better.

Eventually, when I run out of chips, I weave my way back to the hotel. It's the middle of the afternoon, and the sun is absolutely blinding. I need something to drink. Something like water. And a nap. Maybe a massage. Gordo's fingers in my hair, his mouth on my body, until I finally fall asleep and this whole awful situation is a problem for another day.

Gordo's sitting in the lobby bar when I walk in, and relief is so sweet at the sight of him. That is, until he laughs and leans in to speak with the person next to him.

It's Elias.

Motherfucking Emu Elias.

Gordo spots me and he waves, face breaking into a smile.

I don't have time for Elias right now. Will he be coming too? Setting up his emu farm next door to Gordo and his reptile rescue? They look pretty cozy in each other's company. We'll probably see a lot of him back at home.

I can't deal with any of this.

"Bailey?" Gordo calls my name as the elevator door closes.

But I only get a few more seconds of respite because he must take the next one up. I've been in the hotel room long enough to get my shoes and socks off when the lock whirs and Gordo comes in.

"Are you okay?" he says.

"Fine." My head spins and I can't get it to stop.

"You didn't say hi in the bar."

"Had enough already."

He laughs. "Farewell drinks at the retreat?"

"Something like that." My belt is too tight. I fumble to get it off. It doesn't help. I undo my pants too.

"Bailey." Gordo's voice softens and I can't handle that. I need to be angry. I need to get ready for what's coming. Jake the Jerk in my backyard, like we're kids all over again.

I say, "You're spending a lot of time with Elias."

"He's fun."

"Yeah?" I'm pacing in uneven circles. I can't get my breathing to slow down. "How much fun?"

Gordo frowns. "We just talk. He wants to come see the horses."

"I don't care about the fucking horses right now, Gordo."

"Bailey?" He steps toward me, but his hands on my shoulders feel like weights that will crush me, and I shrug him off. "What's going on?"

"You know what's going on." I shake my head. "You were supposed to be here with me. Not chumming up with Elias."

"I thought that was the whole point. Jake was bringing someone, so you needed to too."

"Jeez, thanks. If I need someone to make me feel extra pathetic, I'll call you."

"Bailey." This time, his grip is too strong for me to throw off. "What's wrong? This isn't about Elias. You've hardly said two words to him the whole time we've been here."

"You're on my side," I say.

He kisses me, and I want to push him away. I don't want softness right now.

"I'm always on your side," he says, and his words break me. I pretty much collapse, sinking down onto the giant bed—or at least that's the plan, such as it is, but my angle is wrong and my ass brushes the edge of the mattress before I slide all the way to the ground, banging my tailbone on the bedframe on my way.

"Ow! Fuck!"

Gordo drops to his knees. "Are you okay?"

"No, I'm not fucking okay. Why do you keep asking me that when I am clearly very not okay?"

A gentle tap sounds on the door, and a voice says, "Housekeeping."

"Go away!" I shout, but Gordo does the sensible thing and goes to the door. His soft voice as he makes our apologies grates on my nerves, even though none of this is his fault. When the housekeeper is gone, he comes back, and I expect him to sit down too, but instead he stands in front of me and holds out his hand.

Sighing, I take it and let him pull me to my feet. He walks us down into the living room and sits on the couch, pulling me with him. I resist the urge to crawl into his lap, because I am not a child. I'm about to be the VP of sales for an entire fucking country. The very thought makes me shudder.

Gordo sighs. "So tell me what happened."

And I do. The whole awful conversation. All of them. The one with Ed. The one with Lachlan. The one with Jake yesterday.

"And now he's going to be there. All the time. Checking in on me. Popping in to see how things are going."

"I thought you said his job involved a lot of travel?"

"Four conference calls, Gordo." I wave my fingers in his face so we're clear how many four is exactly. "That's all I had to see him for and maybe one of these weekends every couple years. That was it. And now we're going to be his . . ." I wave some more while I think of the right word. "Home-fucking-base. And you and Elias are all buddy-buddy. We'll be having them over for potlucks and game nights, and I just can't." I drag a forlorn finger along the leather. "I can't, Gordo."

"So quit."

His words are so absurd I laugh, long and loud. But when I glance up at him, he's not even smiling.

"What?"

"Quit."

I pull myself up straight. "Why would I do that?"

He shakes his head incredulously. "Because you hate it? Because it makes you miserable? Because Jake the Jerk manipulated you into this position and—"

"He didn't manipulate me."

"He has, Bailey. Everything you've done, it's been a reaction to something he's done first. This whole weekend—"

"Not everything." I slide a hopeful hand along his thigh, but he's clearly not in the mood.

"What are you getting out of this? Why are you still playing their game?"

Isn't it obvious? "Because it's my job."

"Exactly." He cups my face between his hands. I love it when he does this. "It's a job, Bailey. It's not your identity, and it's causing you more harm than fulfillment."

"And I what? I quit?"

"Exactly. It's not that hard." His smile is soft and encouraging, and I want to believe him so badly, but I can't.

"I'm not like you." I know what he's saying, but he doesn't understand. I climb off the couch and go to the window. The fountains are quiet.

"What do you mean?" Gordo asks.

"I mean I don't have an eight-figure parachute. I can't just quit."

The room goes still.

See? Point made.

"But you have mine."

I close my eyes because those were the words I wanted and the words I can't accept.

"Gordo, no."

"Yes." He comes off the couch to pull me close. "Bailey. Please. It's more money than I know what to do with. Than I'll ever be able to spend. I've tried to do some good with it. Let me do something good for you. Quit. Let me do this for you."

"I can't."

"Why?" He sounds so sad.

"Because if I quit, they win. Jake wins. They wore me down and now I'm leaving with my tail between my legs."

"That's not how it works. If you quit, you stop playing their game. You don't lose; you make your own rules."

But I can't imagine how that happens. Because I'm not Gordo. I'm not going to go on a quest to find myself. I'm not going to start rescuing abandoned orchids and succulents that people can't take care of anymore. And I can't ask him to literally pay my way while I figure it out. That's not fair to either of us, no matter how generous his heart is.

The fountains start up, spewing water in intricate patterns.

I say, "I'm going for a walk."

"I'll come with you."

"No." I hold up a hand. "I need to think."

"Bailey."

"I'll be back in a while. Go have dinner with Elias or something."

15

You can walk for a long time in Las Vegas. I get lost somewhere in Caesar's Palace. I swear I pass the same statue of Zeus or whoever like six times.

What a mess. How does one white lie lead to all this? I needed someone to help me stand up to my childhood bully, and now Gordo's offering to be my sugar daddy and Jake is going to win all the marbles.

I have never not worked. When I was a teenager—around the time Jake moved away, actually—I got a job flipping burgers at a fast-food joint. Dad said it would build up my self-confidence. Jake leaving town did more for that, but that first job earned me some money, and that turned out to be pretty good too. I had part-time gigs all through college. I sold backscratchers at a mall kiosk. I cold-called strangers asking for donations to their alma mater. I was so good at it that they had me training new staff by the end of my second month. I had a job lined up to start the Monday after graduation, and while I've changed companies a few times, I've never been unemployed. I've set sales records everywhere I've worked.

And now Jake the Jerk is going to ruin it all.

I finally grab a cab and get it to take me back to the hotel, because I have no idea where the hell I am. The casinos all start to look the same after a while.

The room is empty when I return. No note from Gordo. I check my texts, and he's only sent one.

Eating with Elias. Let me know when you get back.

But I don't text him because he'll want to talk, and he'll offer the things he already has, and I still can't say yes. No need to talk in circles when I can do the laps in my head.

I order room service. The pulled pork sandwich is divine. The root vegetable fries need to stop being a trend. Sweet potato or death. Parsnip has no business being here.

I spend a little time watching the fountains, but it's not the same without Gordo. Eventually, I pull the blankets around my ears and fall asleep.

Sometime in the middle of the night, I wake up and Gordo's there. Well, sort of. We're back to being friends, apparently. No more snuggle buddies. He's got his back to me, and the space between us on the giant mattress feels cavernous.

I have to quit. Gordo's right. But I can't simply walk away. It would be easy enough to get fired. Jake would see to that. I could sit on my ass for a couple months, and they'd finally let me go, probably with a nice package for my trouble. I don't think my ego could let me do it, though. So what? I work my butt off for Jake and Ed while hustling my contacts for a new job? Go to every networking event I can stand until the right person hands me the right business card and I find my escape hatch?

The questions go around and around, and at some point, I fall asleep again. When I wake up, the bed is empty. So is the room. I lie there for a few minutes, waiting for Gordo to appear with coffee and croissants.

Would it be so bad? Letting Gordo wait on me hand and foot.

He would. Even if he were paying the bills, he'd still be the one making sure I was happy.

And if I'm trying to find a new job, if I'm moving and shaking on top of doing the job I already have, where does Gordo fit into this? Because he's here with me this weekend, but he doesn't want to be my permanent plus-one for every happy hour. That's not who he is. I may have misjudged his sexuality, but I still know him.

In the question of my career or a relationship with Gordo, I'm starting to worry it really is an either-or proposition.

He's not coming back. I've been lying here for thirty minutes and I'm still alone.

I push up on my elbows, and my heart stops.

His bag is gone. His ugly, eyesore Elvis bag, which I thought was a harbinger of things to come when we arrived, isn't on the luggage stand.

He wouldn't leave, would he? Our flight's not for a few more hours. He wouldn't hop in a cab and just go. Or spend one or two of his millions and charter a flight home. I told him I needed space to think, but he wouldn't leave me all alone here, would he?

I check my phone. There's a text from about thirty minutes ago. Maybe the thing that woke me up. All it says is, *We need to talk.*

Yeah. In the light of day, we really do. I text back.

Where are you?

Pool. With Elias.

Ugh. I regret anything I might have insinuated about Elias and Gordo yesterday, but I still don't want to see the Emu man this morning.

Jake?

I get a thumbs up that doesn't tell me anything.

Gordo. Is Jake there?

At least this time he replies with words.

Coast is clear.

I drag my heels getting down there. Jake's a sneaky fucker. If Elias is there, Jake must be waiting in the wings somewhere. I stop and grab a coffee and a muffin, but finally I'm out of ways to procrastinate that don't involve alcohol or losing huge sums of money.

Like yesterday morning, the pool deck is empty. And cold. Jesus, these daily temperature swings are vicious. Gordo and Elias are seated on a couple loungers in one of the few spots the sun has touched. They're both still wearing jackets and have cozy-looking woven blankets wrapped around their knees. Gordo's rhinestone bag is on the ground next to his chair.

"Hey," he says as I approach.

"Good morning." I toast Elias with my coffee, and he waves cheerily at me.

I go to sit down, but Gordo catches my wrist. "No. Come here. It's cold."

And I shouldn't, because we can't get more attached until I know what's going to happen, but I spent all night wanting to touch him, and now he's smiling his soft smile at me, and I'm helpless to resist. So I slide onto the lounger between his spread legs, settling against his chest. He wraps the blanket around us both, and Jesus, this is nice. I can't give this up. No job is worth losing Gordo. He offers way too many benefits.

I nibble on my muffin and listen absently while Elias and Gordo talk about the finer points of emu husbandry. They're such nerds. Elias obviously has appalling taste in men, but otherwise I do see how he'd be a good friend for Gordo.

Also, I keep waiting for him to excuse himself or for Gordo to start dropping subtle hints that he should go so that Gordo and I can talk, but he keeps chatting like somehow we're all a unit now.

As I start to get restless, Gordo says, "Elias has something he needs to tell you."

I tip my head up to glance at him, and he's watching me through all his bushy hair. He's back to his usual self today. Scruffy clothes, scruffy mop hair. I love this version of him so much. The other one, the slick polished one, is impressive. It's seductive. But this one is mine. He bends down to kiss me, and yes, this is my choice. I choose Gordo.

For a second, I forget we have an audience and lean into the kiss. Thank God we have the blanket, because my body is responding to him, and Gordo is either keeping a flashlight in his pocket, or he is very happy to see me too. But eventually, he pulls back, nosing at my jaw until I have to turn my head back toward Elias, who is watching us with a bemused smile.

I sigh. "Whatever it is, say it." I leave the *and then you can go* unsaid, but I hope he gets it.

Elias nods. He says, "Jake is using you."

Please. "Tell me something I don't know. When isn't he using someone?" Probably shouldn't say that out loud to his boyfriend, but I'm done playing nice.

"No," Elias shakes his head. "No, he's really using you. He's trying to save his job."

I sit up straighter. Behind me, Gordo doesn't move, like nothing Elias is saying is a surprise.

"What do you mean?"

"I mean," Elias says slowly, "when they announced the merger, Jake's job was made redundant. Too many layers of management. Not enough efficiency. He was furious. Desperate. He begged. Saw your name on the staff list and said he knew you. That you were the best in the business, and if they kept him on, that he and you would work together to turn things around."

"He said that?" I say. Some perverse part of me, maybe the

preteen part that still lives both in terror and in awe of Jake, thrills at the recognition.

"He did more than say it," Elias says. "He practically wrote a dissertation. He got a tip-off that they were going to let him go, and he spent two days writing up a report on your performance and how he could use it. He had your sales figures, your close rates. He promised if he could keep his job, he'd figure out how you did it and roll it out across the whole company."

My brain cramps as I try to figure out what he's saying. "So he begged his way back in by promising to ride my coattails?"

"He said you were friends from when you were kids. That you'd be unstoppable together."

Something Ed said the day before comes back to me. That Jake had been singing my praises from before the merger closed. Is this what Ed meant? That Jake looked me up like a creepy corporate stalker and then staked his job on my performance.

I glance up at Gordo. "You knew about this?"

"Elias told me last night. I told him how upset you were."

I'm not sure I'm keen on Elias knowing my personal emotional trauma, but if it means revelations like this, I guess I can work with it.

"Your boyfriend is a supreme jackass," I say.

Elias grimaces. "I thought he was just Type A. I'm learning my mistake, trust me."

That snivelling, manipulative, self-obsessed asshole. It's all been a lie, from that first day in the conference room. He wasn't surprised to see me. He'd known I'd be there. Counted on it, in fact, because I was the only one who could save his skin. And here I've been, working my ass off for guys like Lachlan, and it's been Jake in the background pulling the strings the whole time.

I squirm, pulling up to my knees so I can face Gordo. I kiss him with every ounce of my heart. His eyes shine when I pull back. I say, "I love you."

He smiles. "I know."

He's loved me for ages. Looked out for me when I was too stubborn and too worked up to do it myself. In a choice between a career that is doing its best to use me up and spit me out, and a man who cares this much about me, is there actually any choice at all?

"Hey! It's my favourite people."

I turn, and Jake's coming across the pool deck. He's in a polo shirt and khakis and looks like the human embodiment of an upwardly mobile vacation. He waves like he doesn't have a care in the world.

Well, he's about to.

I move so fast, Gordo doesn't have time to catch me.

"Bailey." His voice is full of warning, but I don't care. I march across the deck. Jake's all happy smiles and confidence as I stride toward him.

"Morning, buddy," he says. "I meant to ask you if you want Lachlan's old office, or if you think I could have it?"

He doesn't even see his doom until I have his shirt in two fists. Anger is pretty powerful. I spin him until he's got his back to the pool.

"Hey. Hey, what's up?" He grapples for purchase as I lean him back.

I get close to his face so there's no question of him mishearing. Between clenched teeth, I say, "Fuck you. And both our jobs."

Then I let him go.

Teenage me is so proud.

His face, as he tumbles into the water, is priceless. I will remember it forever. Gordo and Elias both rise to their feet. Elias looks astonished. Gordo looks proud.

Jake comes up, spluttering and wiping his face. He's soaked and his clothes cling to him.

"What the hell?" he says.

"You know exactly what." I jab a finger at him. "You are a jerk and a loser and you always have been. I'm not playing your game anymore, Jake. Sink on your own. I quit."

He spits and splashes. "What? You can't quit. Bailey."

It's hard to take him seriously as he wades to the edge of the pool. He looks like a wet cat, and about as happy.

"I'll have my resignation in your inbox by the end of the day. And I'll be sure to cc Ed so there's no confusion."

Gordo comes to my side and I slip an arm around him. He puts one of his on my shoulders and kisses my temple.

"Good choice," he says.

I laugh as we turn. Jake's still yelling from the pool. Some of the staff have come to see what the commotion is, but Jake is no longer my problem, and a fully dressed man in the water is nowhere near the weirdest thing they've ever seen at a Vegas hotel.

I nuzzle into Gordo's side. "Easiest choice ever."

So it turns out, when you're unemployed and your boyfriend is a top-secret millionaire, things like airline change fees suddenly don't seem like such a hassle. I'm going to do my best not to get too spoiled, but when Gordo suggests we stay a few more days, I jump on it.

"I thought you didn't like Vegas?" I say.

He lifts me up so I have to wrap my legs around his hips. Did I mention I'm naked? So is he. No one's going anywhere.

"I like it wherever you are."

His kiss makes me melt, which is good, because I need to be butter a few minutes later when he has me facedown on the bed and he's slowly sliding into me.

"Oh, Jesus. Gordo." My knuckles go white as I grip the sheets.

"Too much?"

Never. Gordo is everything I want.

We don't get out of bed all day.

Well. We take advantage of the shower a few times.

"What do you think about putting one of these nozzles in the condo?" I say.

"Whatever you want," he says.

We sleep through dinner and order room service at two in the morning.

"Gordo," I say as I chew on a french fry.

"Yeah?" He opted for a club sandwich and is currently picking out the middle slice of bread from each quarter, which, if you ask me, defeats the whole point of a club sandwich.

"Did you change our room booking?"

He freezes halfway through his sandwich surgery. "What do you mean?"

The question is casual, but he's only wearing his shorts, and a flush creeps up his chest, barely visible under his hair.

Busted.

I can barely control my smile. "I mean, I called after you agreed to come on this trip and made sure the room had two beds. It was a whole thing, so I know I did it, and then they emailed me the confirmation. But I also put your name on the reservation. So did you call them after and ask them for a room with one bed?"

"No."

"Oh." That's disappointing. Here I had visions of Gordo planning to seduce me all along and sneakily calling to make sure we had no option but to sleep together, and it turns out maybe I was getting ahead of myself.

"But I called and asked them to upgrade from the room

block to a suite, and they said the last one available only had one bed."

Sneaky bastard.

"So your plan was to get into my bed all along?"

He shrugs. "I wanted you to have a nice time. If you had to come and deal with all this awful stuff at work, I wanted to make sure you were sleeping well."

And I have definitely done that. Well, most nights.

"You're so thoughtful," I say.

His sandwich seems to meet with his specifications because he puts a wedge in his mouth like it's meant to be bite-size. I guess for Gordo it is.

He licks mayo off his thumb. "And that's why I got the first-class plane tickets too."

I drop a fry in my lap. "The what?"

He smiles. "You didn't think we kept getting magical upgrades because of your good looks?"

"Uh. Yeah." God, I was so strung out that afternoon at the airport I could hardly function. So yeah, I'd assumed the first-class thing was good karma.

Instead, it was Gordo.

One more thought shakes loose in my head. "What about the condo?"

That catches him off guard at least. He frowns his bushy frown. "What about it?"

I choose my words carefully. "I mean, I think we've established that you don't actually need a roommate. Financially speaking. Why don't you have a place of your own?"

He buys time with another quarter sandwich, chewing carefully. "I was lonely. The people I'd been closest to were the ones I worked with, and then we weren't really speaking to each other without lawyers present. And everyone else . . . When you . . . Something changes when you get a lot of money like that. It changes how people relate to you. But you didn't. You thought I was just a guy who needed a place to live." He pushes the plate with his sandwich aside and reaches for me. "And I could tell you needed someone too. Just took you two years to realize it."

I shake my head as I crawl into his lap to kiss him. "I don't deserve you."

"But you got me," he says.

With full bellies, we get back into bed. I'm too spent to fuck, but I could crawl on top of Gordo and let him wrap me up like a Bailey burrito forever.

He says, "Bailey."

"Yeah?" I yawn.

"I booked us a helicopter ride in the morning."

Fine by me. "To see the Grand Canyon? That's the kind of thing people do out here."

"No. To see the mustangs. I had to make a lot of phone calls, but I found a guy who was willing to take us that far north. Turns out it's a long way from here. But Bailey, I was thinking. There have to be horses that need rescuing at home. We could get some land, north of the city, maybe a farm. Elias might know someone. What do you think?"

I snuggle in closer. "Whatever you want to do, I'm with you." Time for sleep. I'm done fighting. Regardless of what the future holds for us—and it will no doubt feature a menagerie of horses, lizards, snakes and turtles, along with special appearances by lost chihuahuas, the occasional emu, and maybe a few orchids that people don't want anymore—I'm confident Gordo knows what we're doing. He may be a man of few words, but he is a man with a plan. I can trust in that.

EPILOGUE

A hairless dog is not the weirdest thing I've seen this week. And no, before you ask, it's not intentionally hairless. Not one of those designer dogs with the floofy feet and wispy ears. Maggie the pug-corgi cross has definitely seen better days, if the crusty scabs the mange has left on her poor skinny body are any indication.

I understand now why Gordo doesn't bother with nice clothes. A python is far less likely to puke on you than a puppy, but when you're cleaning up after animals all day, dry-clean only becomes a thing of the past.

"Come on, pretty girl," I say, scooping her up. "Let's get you clean."

I'm getting good at these medicated baths. Maggie's been here on the farm with us for the last week, and I admit she was in such rough shape that I could barely bring myself to look at her when she arrived. Now I want to kiss her smooshy face and tell her she's going to make the other dogs so jealous when her hairs all grow back in. She's got the best eyes ever. Dark brown like chocolate, and when they stare up at me, I can see so much gratitude and love.

A door opens down the hall, followed by the stomping of boots, no doubt to knock the snow off.

"Bailey?" Gordo calls.

"Back here." My answer is almost drowned out by the chorus of barking dogs that greet Gordo. We have twelve dogs staying with us right now. Most of them have free run of the house because Gordo says they need to be socialized. Maggie, we're keeping separate until her skin starts to improve. I think the isolation is harder on me than it is on her, but when I suggest I could wrap her up in one of those baby carriers and take her everywhere with me, Gordo said it was a dog, and if I wanted a baby, we should talk.

I'm pretty sure he was joking about that last part. I'm still learning Gordo's sense of humour, but his beard does this little wiggle when he's trying not to laugh, and it definitely wiggled when he said the b-word.

I do not want a baby. My life has already gone through enough upheaval. Plus, who the hell is going to take care of a baby on top of the dozen dogs, four houses, six snakes, fifteen lizards, and however many turtles we're up to this week?

The day Jake the Jerk stood at the head of the conference table and told us our jobs were all safe, I could not have seen this coming.

Gordo and I bought the farm in the fall. And I mean *we* bought the farm. It's surprising how much money you can get for selling a two-plus bedroom condo downtown and how far that money will go as soon as you leave the city limits. Gordo offered to finance the whole thing himself, but I wanted to know it was ours from the outset, so we split the cost of the property, and I've done my best to contribute as we fixed up the place.

Not that it's a real farm. Or not all of a farm. Pretty sure some farmer got talked into selling his land to a developer who sees the creeping market for mega homes up here, but he kept forty-some acres for himself for a few more years, before eventually selling that to us. Fortunately, we don't want a mega home. Or at least, not like the cookie-cutter mansions going in down the street. The old farmhouse was perfect . . . with a few additions.

I know the locals talk about us. The two gay guys who bought the old property, fixed up the barn, and turned it into an animal sanctuary. The wiring Gordo had to have done so he could run heating lamps for all the reptiles alone definitely started more than a few rumours that we were setting up a grow op. But it's Canada. Even if that was what we were doing, we don't need to be sneaky about stuff like that. Gordo's cupcakes are very popular when we have the neighbours over.

And I've heard Gordo chatting with people in the little café whenever we run into town for supplies. I know he's tried to explain pansexuality and demisexuality to them. A few even get it. The guy who runs the coffee shop is bi. We're going to try to introduce him to Elias, who is coming to visit next month.

"Hey, pretty girl," Gordo says.

"Hi yourself," I say, then laugh when I realize he's talking to Maggie. She wiggles her whole body as he brushes a hand over her head. Every animal we've brought here over the last few months loves him. I don't know what it is.

Or maybe I do. Gordo's always exuded this calm steadiness. I react to it as much as the dogs and horses and bearded dragons do. I always have, I just didn't understand why. Everyone wants to love Gordo, and for him to love them, from the minute he walks into your life. And I happen to be the lucky sonofabitch who gets to do it every day.

The thing is, except when I have to get up at three in the morning to bottle feed a litter of abandoned puppies, I don't miss my old life at all. I thought I'd miss the excitement, the thrill of working those connections, of building relationships with prospects so they trust you and keep coming back. But only a handful of them reached out when I left BGS&M, and none have been in touch again, even when I invited them to our adoption open house.

Turns out my old life was seriously lonely. Without Gordo in it, I probably would have started sleeping at the office ages before Jake the Jerk ever showed up on the scene.

I wish I could say I never heard about Jake again after Vegas. But since Gordo and Elias are pretty much BFFs now, I'd basically have to permanently stick my head in the puppy pile to make that true. The good news is the end of Jake's time at the company happened before he and Elias even made it on their plane. My resignation letter was short and to the point, and I don't know if Ed meant to cc me on his reply or not, but it was succinct.

Jack, clean out your desk tomorrow.

Elias's departure from Team Jake was a done deal by the time they landed.

And I shouldn't revel in someone else's downfall, but come on. It's Jake the Jerk. He outed me and never once apologized for it, then thought he could ride my coattails back into Ed's good graces. He was never going to list me as a reference as he tries to rebuild his career, so it's okay if I dance around the rubble.

"I think she's rinsed," Gordo says in my ear. I glance down, and Maggie is shivering in the sink as I let warm water pour over her skin.

"Oh, I'm so sorry. Sorry, pretty good girl. You're such a good patient girl. I'm so sorry." I babble as I lift her out and dry her off. She's so quiet and patient. I can't wait to see if she comes out of her shell as she gets better and learns to trust us more, or if she's always going to be this sweet, stoic girl. I have a feeling Maggie will be a foster fail and stay with us permanently, but I haven't told Gordo yet.

After I get Maggie settled and go back to the main part of the house, I find Gordo in the living room. He's feeding a bearded dragon—this one is called Hector—a cricket clasped between tweezers, and while I love our new life, I could still do without this part. I go to the kitchen and get dinner started.

Turns out Gordo is a terrible cook. He's a great baker—he's talking about selling fresh sourdough at the farmer's market this summer—but he sucks at making actual meals. All the time we lived together, I assumed we lived on ramen and takeout because I didn't have time to sit before I'd be back on my computer, scheduling calls and hunting up new connections. Turns out Gordo didn't know how to make anything else.

We're working on it. So far, we've learned to make chicken pot pie and chicken à la king, and last week we made chicken king pie because we didn't have enough ingredients for either. It was still pretty tasty.

I've pulled up a recipe for cabbage rolls that I found on Pinterest last week, and I'm getting the ground pork out of the fridge when I realize Gordo is looming in the kitchen doorway.

"Jesus, don't scare me." I put a hand to my chest. He smiles softly, but he doesn't budge. I tug at my T-shirt self-consciously. "What?"

"You move differently," he says.

I flush at the idea he's been watching me. He watched me for so long and I never realized, but now that I know, I can't help the way it gets my blood stirring.

"What do you mean?"

He takes his time as he pushes off the doorframe. His steps are deliberate and his gaze is on me the whole way across the kitchen floor. It's like being stalked by a gentle predator, and I am rock hard by the time he folds me in his arms and kisses me.

"You used to rush through the condo like a frightened bird. Like if you ever landed, something would eat you. You don't move like that anymore. You're taking space. Time. It's good to see."

I snort. "I wouldn't mind if you ate me."

He lifts me up, the way he knows I love. "That can be arranged."

I purr as I wrap my knees around his hips and tangle my fingers in his hair. "What about dinner?"

"There's ramen in the cupboard."

I was sort of looking forward to cabbage rolls. But not as much as I'm looking forward to Gordo devouring me.

"Did you check on the horses?" I ask as he carries me upstairs.

"Yes."

"Dogs are fed?"

"Dogs are all fed."

"Did you check the drip in the chameleon's—" But I don't get to finish as I'm launched airborne and thump down on the mattress with a laugh, which quickly gets smothered as Gordo covers my body with his.

His thumb on my bottom lip is delicious. His lips on my temple are divine. The promise of what will be coming soon— me! I'll be coming soon!—as he grinds against my hip makes me shiver.

He says, "Are you happy?"

I wrap my arms around his neck. "Absolutely."

"Do you miss it? Before?"

I pause. He's never asked me quite so directly before. I make sure to look him right in the eye so he knows I'm serious. "Not in the least."

His smile is a rainbow. He kisses each of my eyebrows. My cheeks. My mouth.

He says, "I love you, Bailey."

"I know."

It's our thing. Han and Leia. Gordo's a fan of Scarlet Johansson, but he's a huge Star Wars nerd. We've watched all the movies. Prequels. Sequels. Spin-offs. Cartoons. I'm not sure I understand it all, but then I don't understand the magic that brought Gordo into my life either, and I've learned it's best not to question it. Don't look a gift horse in the mouth and all that. We have plenty of other horses to look after.

"Bailey," Gordo says as he kisses my throat.

"Yeah?"

"When Elias comes to visit, maybe we can talk about adding an emu rescue?"

I love that he always phrases these things like questions. As if I'm going to say no. As if I don't go along with every single idea he has. As if there are many emus to rescue in and around Toronto, but that's not the point. I love that he asks.

"Whatever you want," I say.

I would do anything for this man. Being with him is the only benefit I need.

ABOUT THE AUTHOR

Whether I knew it then or not, I've been a writer since the second grade, when I wrote a short story about a girl and her horse. My grandmother typed it out for me and said she'd never seen so many quotation marks from a seven-year-old before. I took that as a challenge and have tried to break that record in all the stories I've taken on since then. It's good to have goals, right?

I live in Toronto with my very patient husband and the world's goofiest rescue dog. I try to split my time between writing, community theatre stage management, and traveling anywhere that has good wine. Tragically, this leaves no time to clean the house.

ALSO BY ALLISON TEMPLE

Out & About
Work-Love Balance
Honeymoon Sweet

The Seacroft Stories
Top Shelf
Cold Pressed
Hot Potato

Standalone
The Pick Up